CW00781532

| SUNDERLAND CITY LIBRARIES | |
|---|---|
| K3535388007 | |
| Bertrams | 15/09/2009 |
| FRI | £5.99 |
| WTC | PO-3044 |

# Style Sisters

# California Crush

## Liz Elwes

PICCADILLY PRESS • LONDON

*To my parents – for everything.*
*To the fabulous writer Cathy Hopkins – whose generosity*
*and kindness is legendary, I will be ever grateful.*
*To Giles Elwes and my children William, Alice, Thomas and Jamie*
*for having such interesting lives and giving me so many lines*
*in the book (I hope you don't mind).*
*To my own style sisters: Frances Toynbee, Sarah Mower,*
*Jill Rothwell, Mary Saldanha, Marion Jeffrey, Anne Rands,*
*Rosie and Olivia McDonnell and Suzanne Vandevelde.*
*To Clare Elwes. To Johnny, Christine and Anne-Marie.*
*To Brenda Gardner, Ruth Williams, Melissa Hyder and*
*everyone at Piccadilly for their help, patience and guidance.*
*To Bernice Green who started it.*

First published in Great Britain in 2009
by Piccadilly Press Ltd,
5 Castle Road, London NW1 8PR
www.piccadillypress.co.uk

Text copyright © Liz Elwes, 2009

All rights reserved. No part of this publication may be
reproduced, stored in a retrieval system, or transmitted
in any form or by any means electronic, mechanical,
photocopying, recording or otherwise, without the
prior permission of the copyright owner.

The right of Liz Elwes to be identified as Author of this work
has been asserted by her in accordance with the
Copyright, Designs and Patents Act, 1988

A catalogue record for this book is available
from the British Library

ISBN: 978 1 85340 986 8 (paperback)

1 3 5 7 9 10 8 6 4 2

Printed and bound in Great Britain by CPI Bookmarque Ltd
Cover design by Simon Davis

**Mixed Sources**
Product group from well-managed
forests and other controlled sources
www.fsc.org Cert no. TT-COC-002227
© 1996 Forest Stewardship Council

# Chapter 1

**Tuesday 7.00 a.m.**

Look at the time!

It is barely dawn!

And there are at least two reasons why I don't want to be awake this early.

1. I am still on my summer holidays.

2. I was dreaming about gorgeous, brilliant actor Gregg Madison.

OK, three reasons.

3. Mum is in a funny mood.

A 'stop lying around and do something' mood. Which, as every teenager knows, is the most tedious kind.

She says she is going to find something for me to do today.

I don't know what it might be, but you can bet it's not going to make a girl want to spring out of bed with a whoop tearing off her jimmy-jams.

I'm also having quite a struggle managing this pen (the one with the wobbly pink heart on a spring on the top) *and* this diary. This is because I am trying to write with a pillow clamped around my ears. I have fashioned it myself and it is quite bonnet-like. I fancy it makes me look like an extra in a Jane Austen TV series (though I appreciate this may be open to debate).

The reason for this headgear is because only a few metres away from my bedroom door I can hear the bellowing of a large animal in distress. Its mournful groans are echoing around the house.

Dad is singing in the shower.

I know he is doing it on purpose. He is bitter because he is the only member of our family not still on holiday, so he wants the rest of us to know that *he's* had to get up. But I say if he wanted to idle about all summer he should have been a teacher like Mum. Because she's deputy head at my school, she's been whiling away the time since we got back from California – mainly by snooping on the new family who moved in opposite while we were away. On second thoughts, an image of Dad telling one of his 'jokes' to a group of Boughton High Year Sevens (especially that new joke which involves him rolling up a trouser leg) flashes into my mind. A dread chill sweeps over me.

If I could just manage to get back to sleep again (fat chance with that noise coming from the shower) it would also mean at least half an hour less of today. Which I already know will be rivalling yesterday for the title Most Boring Day of the Summer Holidays.

Since we returned from holiday a week ago, no one knows better than me that *that* contest is turning into *quite* a fight. With everyone remotely interesting still away, to say I am living the quiet life would be an understatement.

I cannot wait till my friends get back from their holidays. And my heavenly boyfriend Jack. Jack and me. Chloe and Tom. Best friends dating best friends. It's perfect. Thank goodness they will be returning soon and we can get back to how things were. I can't stand the wait much longer.

Dad has stopped singing. Blissful peace. I can cast aside my pillow-bonnet.

It is 7.20 a.m. I am going to try to get back to sleep for at least another hour. Or even better still, until Rani arrives. Is it possible to sleep for three or four days? I'm going for it . . .

## 7.30 a.m.

Trouble is, I've never been a girl who can fall back to sleep once she's woken up.

No. Not me. I can lie on my bed, close the curtains, pull the duvet over my head and screw my eyes tight shut, but however hard I try, my brain hums away in background. Bit like the fridge in our kitchen. I can't sleep on journeys either, which was very boring on the long flight back from Los Angeles. Ned was out like a light as soon as he sat down, in his irritating younger brother way, but my nose was pressed against the window or observing my fellow passengers, like a meerkat surveying the plains. Eyes wide.

## 7.58 a.m.

To while away some more time in bed and avoid Mum, who will try and get me involved in spying on our new neighbours – or 'just being friendly' as she calls it – I reached out for the little mirror I keep on my bedside table and:

1. Checked out my new spot. Yes, delighted to see it still proudly shining on my chin. I must remember to offer my services to anyone in the neighbourhood requiring a witch.

2. Dabbed my face with a used tea bag. I brought it up last night on a saucer. I should have sat up for this. A dribble went in

my ear. Officially I should have a bath in strong tea every day. Chloe said she heard it worked to keep your skin a golden colour after your holiday. I am rather nervous of fake tan after a previous unfortunate experience. Sadly the golden colour of the bathwater got on the towels as well as me and, after a short but meaningful discussion, Mum and I agreed that the total-immersion-in-tea idea would have to be abandoned.

3. I have also worked out it is exactly six days and three hours since we stepped off the plane from Los Angeles, California, the United States of America! Where I have just had the best holiday *of my life*.

## 8.15 a.m.
Had to pause for a moment as the springy heart on my pen fell off and pinged across the room. This is good, as the novelty of the constant wibbly-wobbling soon wears off. Yes. Back for not quite a whole week and it has poured with rain every day since we returned. I have even been forced into talking to Ned. We are like those kids in *The Cat in the Hat*, but before the Cat comes along and makes things interesting.

List of things I miss about California:

1. Sun.

2. Gregg Madison, star of the outstanding TV series, *Hollywood High*. OK. So I didn't exactly meet him. But I miss being in the same *country* as him. Totally gorgeous.

For probably the only time in his life, Ned justified his existence and landed a small part in an American TV series. Which was the reason we were all in California in the first place. Dad had a personality transplant and said wildly, 'Let's all go!' And we did. I was convinced I'd get to meet Gregg while Ned was filming. Ned was in the series that's not coming out in Britain till next summer, but because fate is *so* often against me, Gregg Madison mysteriously wasn't in it. And when I nagged and nagged Ned to ask at the studio, he said they told him Gregg was 'out of town'. I got to see the *last* series though, the one that Gregg *was* in. It was on every morning and evening in my hotel room, and now I won't have to wait till next month when it comes over here and I will be able to annoy everyone at school by telling them what happens. And I know everything that happens in the series after *that* too (Ned is *so* rubbish at keeping secrets). How popular will *I* be?

Now where was I? Oh yes. Great things about LA.

3. Santa Monica beach.

4. The hotel pool.

5. Best mates Maddy (not at all jealous that she's American) and Chloe, both being there too. And I am not at all jealous that Maddy took Chloe on holiday with her and that when *my* family left to come back home, Chloe still had more than a *week* to go. Well, I am, but then Chloe's mum was going to have to work all summer and her brother Jim had gone on a camp with the other Down's syndrome children from his special school so she would have had no holiday at all if she *hadn't* gone with Maddy. *And* Chloe is the nicest sister to Jim and friend to *me* in the world and so she did really deserve a break. She must have missed Tom like mad though. They are like twin souls and have been together forever.

6. Best mate Maddy's stunning Malibu beach house. How

brilliant to have a dad who's American. And a world-famous fashion expert and stylist to the TV and film industry. Absolutely no danger of trouser leg raising *there*. His work means Maddy is staying out there for ages. I take it back, I *am* jealous of her.

7. Sun.

8. Cool shops.

9. Gorgeous-looking people (especially boys – and especially TV stars. *Not* that I really noticed that much . . . hem hem. My heart is true to my lovely boyfriend Jack).

10. Frosted cup cakes.

11. Frozen yogurt in heavenly flavours.

12. Sun.

13. And lastly, did I mention Gregg Madison?

This is not being unfaithful to Jack. I cannot wait to see my funny, sharp and good-looking boyfriend when he comes back from his trip to Thailand with his shopaholic mum and her new man.

I am not a child. I know the difference between real love and appreciating the talents of an incredibly good-looking person who you will never meet. (Though I might have at least had a chance if Ned had made more of an effort trying to find out where Gregg Madison was and if Dad had let us stay in LA for a bit longer. But they were deaf to my pleas.)

Writing that list has not cheered me up. It has not cheered me up at all. In fact, I feel quite depressed now. Let's try another list. Reasons to be glad to be home in Moulton village, Near Middleton, Middle of England, Great Britain:

Duh!

NONE.

 CARRIE'S TIP: • • • • • • • • • • • • • • • • • •
If your skin starts tingling in warning that a spot is about
to rear its ugly head and ruin your life, apply spot cream
to the area before it has a chance to appear. If it's
already arrived, apply spot cream, a mud mask or even
toothpaste before you go to bed. It should be a lot smaller
in the morning!

# Chapter 2

Another day dawns in the dreariest corner in the country of Drear.

Mum is yelling up the stairs. I will not answer.

Yesterday's task was to go round to the new neighbours and take them some Neighbourhood Watch leaflets.

Yes.

Brilliant.

Welcome to your new neighbourhood: *Burglar City*.

Actually, the last crime committed in Moulton was probably a witch-ducking in the pond. As I was shoving the leaflets through the letterbox Mrs Banks, the lady who has just moved in, opened the door, which was pretty embarrassing. I had to introduce myself. Turns out she's really nice and said that Mum had mentioned me and she was sure her daughter would love to meet me when she got back from visiting her gran in a few days. As I know their daughter is ten years old I think I can cope with the wait. There is an older brother who also seems to be away but Mum seemed to think he's Ned's age, so dead loss all round really.

*10.30 a.m.*

Just been downstairs. Mum's yelling as well as me being starving broke my spirit. I shouldn't have bothered to get up. I am not even allowed to *talk* about rain any more. After an innocent remark from Ned, Mum has forbidden us to talk about the wet stuff that falls out of the sky.

'It hasn't rained *all* the time,' Mum snapped. 'It's only been raining here since . . . since . . . about . . .' and then she went blank.

'Tudor times?' Ned offered, and that did it.

'You two should be ashamed of yourselves!' she yelled. 'You've just had three weeks in Los Angeles – *three weeks*! Sunshine every day, swimming pools, a lovely hotel, and now we're back all you can do is *complain*. Carrie, how I *wish* you had been in time to get a place helping Miss Lamb on her summer drama course. It would have been just the thing to keep you occupied in the mornings . . .'

Miss Lamb teaches drama at our school and she runs an arts and drama course every summer for children from the local primary. Usually it's only girls who go, apart from Jeremy Pratt, who loves any excuse to get pink tights on. Mum, being deputy head of the secondary school most of them will go to, feels an educational kinship with this project and knows way too much about it. The course always ends with a panto-style performance at Moulton Fair. Mum was thrilled that this year, at fourteen, I was at last old enough to volunteer my services and she had nagged and nagged me to offer my help. Like Rani's mum had nagged *her* – she and Miss Lamb are both heavily involved with the local amateur dramatic society.

However, this year Rani and I had ingeniously held back on volunteering until we heard that Miss Lamb had all the help she needed. Somehow dealing with the demands and tantrums of some of the prima donnas that we knew would be participating sounded way too much like hard work. And this year we knew for sure that Jet's younger sister, Donna, was going. Rani and I knew Donna's reputation already. How could we not? We live in such a small place. With her henchwoman Shanaid, no one at Woodside Primary was safe from Donna's scathing remarks. So she was very like her big sister Jet really, whose nastiness and general rudeness is a blot on our harmonious Year Nine group at Boughton High.

After Miss Lamb told us that we had come too late and she had all the help she needed, thank you, we had been able to skip back to our mums, faking deep disappointment, shake our heads and sigh, 'We *tried* . . .'

'I *tried*, Mum . . .' I said now (in excellent whining tone).

But Mum wasn't finished. 'You've got weeks of summer left. You must be able to find *something* interesting to do!'

Ned and I both stared at her again.

'There's *loads* to do!' she responded wildly, glancing at me and adding quickly, 'And that does not include watching more re-runs of *Hollywood High*.'

Which was so unfair, as *Hollywood High* is a quality programme and extremely educational about Beverly Hills youth culture, and anyway I'd cut down to only three episodes a day. (I had brought the latest box set back with me.)

'Oh, for goodness' sake,' Mum barked. 'Use your imagination, read a book.'

'Read 'em,' I replied, quick as a flash.

'What? Every single one?'

She saw me open my mouth and continued speedily, 'In the *world*?'

I shut it again.

'Go to the library. Get some more. I've got some books that need returning anyway. It'll give you something to do and then lots to read until your friends get back.'

And that is the reason she's yelling *again* up the stairs right this moment. That is my task for the day. Middleton library. Which is *so* un-*Hollywood High*.

Where is my pillow-bonnet?

## 11.00 a.m.

It is now official. My social life is at an all-time low. Not only am I reduced to leafleting the neighbours but also, before I could exit the house for the thrills of the library, Jackie Harper, head of our school's *Doctor Who* appreciation society, phoned me to ask me on a trip to Alton Towers.

'I've been researching the rides and I've worked out that three won't be such a good number and I know that Rani, Maddy and Chloe are away. Statistically speaking four will work better.'

*Thanks Jackie,* I thought to myself. When you put it like that – how can I refuse?

'Sorry, Jackie, *really* kind of you to ask.' (*Not.*) 'But Rani, Chloe *and* Maddy will be back then so I won't be able to come with you.' Thinking secretly to myself, *Yes, I do have a social life, thank you. I am not yet Nancy No-Mates, so look elsewhere for someone to make up your numbers.*

'That's a pity,' she sighed. 'That's *six* people I've called already;

I've nearly rung *everyone* on my list. Never mind. Anyway, call me if you change your mind.'

Six! That means that there were *five* people, *five* people that Jackie had phoned before me. Jackie, the leader of a group of girls whose idea of a good time is to meet up in their bedrooms and quote whole episodes of *Doctor Who* at each other. I suspect they make cyber helmets and weapons out of tin foil and kitchen roll tubes too, but I can't swear on it.

When I put the phone down, Mum appeared from nowhere, like she does, and asked who it was. Just like that. She has some serious boundary issues. Privacy means nothing to her.

'That's nice,' she murmured when I told her (sometimes I'm too weak to fight).

'No it's not, they were desperate! They only invited me to make up numbers. They're really nice girls, but let's just say our interests differ. They write *Time Lords Rule* on their files and have Tardis pencil cases.'

Mum nodded. 'I see,' and her eyes slid to where I had absent-mindedly doodled *Gregg Madison* on the horoscope section of the newspaper. Which as anyone knows is not the same thing AT ALL.

'That was just an idle doodle.' I sighed. 'You wouldn't understand.'

Mum picked up the paper and scanned the page. 'It says here an exciting stranger from overseas will enter your life.'

I went, 'Ha! Yeah, right.'

'You *might* meet your exciting stranger from afar at the library.'

I sighed deeply.

Everyone knows that the only thing that comes from afar in Middleton library is Mrs Brigstock's body odour. I must have said that out loud because Mum shrieked, 'For goodness' sake, Carrie, how rude. Get your raincoat. I will not have you stuck here complaining for a *second* longer. Get out. Get out. Get out.'

Which wasn't a very nice thing to say to your only daughter. And surely the kind of insensitive treatment that could be very damaging to a girl's self-esteem. Take note, Dr Jennings – my imaginary future therapist.

So I'm off as soon as I find an umbrella.

Everyone knows that horoscopes are rubbish.

 RANI'S TIP: • • • • • • • • • • • • • • • • • • • •

There's not a whole lot we can do about other people's B.O., but stay fresh yourself by using anti-perspirant in the mornings, and giving yourself a once-over with your favourite body spray or perfume on your pulse points. Remember, don't over do it – double takes are flattering, but you don't want to leave people choking in your wake.

# Chapter 3

## Wednesday 3.30 p.m.

I met my stranger from abroad! Horoscopes are now officially true and to be believed at all times.

It didn't go *quite* as I might have imagined. The stranger wasn't *exactly* what I had had in mind, but the main thing was: SOMETHING HAPPENED.

At first everything was going as I had expected on the Most Boring Day of the Summer Holidays. I had to wait ages for the bus in the pouring rain, my umbrella blew inside out – it's *August* for goodness' sake – and by the time I got into the library, hair in rats' tails and clothes gently steaming, I was not in my best mood.

*Why* don't I live in California? Life is so unfair.

Mrs Brigstock spotted me standing in the doorway from behind the battlements of her desk. Her eyes spoke to me as they took in my dripping form. And they did not say 'Welcome'.

Not that you want to rush up to Mrs Brigstock anyway – the body odour can then overwhelm. Experience has taught most people to advance slowly and with caution, so by the time you've reached her desk your nostrils have had time to get used to it. Her hostile stare got worse after I had edged my way across the carpet. Trying not to breathe through my nose, I pulled out the first book from my wet plastic bag and plonked it on the counter.

She snapped it open and peered at the date stamp. 'Overdue.' She sniffed, slightly cheered.

'I know. They all are,' I admitted sheepishly. Even Mum had looked like she thought her library idea wasn't quite that brilliant when she was counting out the cash this morning.

Mrs Brigstock looked up, triumphant. 'There's a big fine to pay on these.'

'I know. Thank goodness they can't lock you up for it yet,' I joked, rummaging in my bag.

Mrs Brigstock gave me a look which said that prison sentences for overdue books would be her dream come true.

'Hi, gorgeous,' a voice said next to me. 'Any chance you could tell me where I could find anything on Robin Hood?'

Mrs Brigstock's head shot up. I turned round and we both found ourselves looking at an extremely short, round boy about eleven or twelve years old. His small pale blue eyes were staring straight at me with a disturbing leer. I took a step back, taking in his red Bermuda shorts and tropical flowers shirt. But that wasn't the most curious thing about him. It was his voice. He was American! In Middleton library.

*This* was my exciting stranger from abroad. Like I said, not exactly what I had imagined. But if I was unsure that he was my destiny, he certainly wasn't unsure that I was his. His eyes never left my face, or any of the blonde, extremely tall, pipecleaner-legged spot-on-chin rest of me. And then to add insult to injury he *winked* at me. Yuck!

'Are you resident? *Locally?*' Mrs Brigstock sniffed again.

The boy tore his gaze away and answered, 'No. Well, kind of, but if I could join, you know, temporarily, I need some books for a . . . a . . . high school project . . .'

'Noo noo noo!' Mrs Brigstock's head shook from side to side with her favourite word. 'This library is for local residents only, not for . . .' She looked the boy up and down. ' . . . Tourists.'

He looked pretty annoyed at this, and who could blame him. Charm is not Mrs Brigstock's thing.

'You may come in and look at books in the library for *reference*,' Mrs Brigstock went on. 'But you can't take any out.'

'I don't think that would really work.' The boy looked around with an exasperated air. 'I mean, my mom would have to bring me every day and I'm not sure —'

*Thud!* Mrs B slammed the cover of the last book on my pile. 'Well, I can't help you, then.' It was obvious that as far as she was concerned, the conversation was over.

'What? You're kidding!' the boy gasped, shocked. 'OK, could you let me just go *see* . . .?' The boy pointed a pudgy finger at the rows and rows of books stretching behind the solid barrier of Mrs Brigstock and her desk. Mrs Brigstock made a grumbling sound and jabbed her finger on a button. I indicated to the bemused boy that he should go through the barrier before Mrs B changed her mind. Even she couldn't stop someone *looking* at the books, though I'm sure it would be her dream for that to be against the law too.

I handed my money over the desk and reluctantly followed him in. Mum would go mental if I didn't come back with at least a few titles from the list of books she'd handed me.

'Hello,' a voice purred in my ear in Teen Fiction.

I looked up, startled, into the grinning features of my new admirer.

'Hi,' I replied. It was a bit of a guarded response. It wasn't exactly the 'Hi' of someone who wanted to be your best friend, but it wasn't totally 'Eurghh! Go away.' I am a kind person and ready to give anyone the benefit of the doubt. Besides, he was American. And might have older friends.

'I'm Gus, by the way. What's your name?'

I told him.

'Look, Carrie, honey, I got a real problem here,' he whined. 'I have *got* to get these books. And I mean *got* to.' He leaned right into my face, and tears began to well up into his eyes. 'It's kind of life or death you know . . . They're not really for me, they're for my big brother, but he . . . he can't come in here . . .' He put his fist to his mouth as if to keep back a sob.

'Why not?' I asked.

'So ill . . .' A tear ran down a chubby cheek. 'Didn't want to tell that . . . woman on the desk. Too personal.'

'Oh my God,' I gasped.

'Just not got long to go . . . kind of a last-wish thing . . .'

'Look,' I blurted out. 'If you want to borrow some books so badly, I could take them out for you on my card, and on my mum's too. I can take out five books on each.'

A smile momentarily lit his face, but then he frowned. 'How would that work?'

'Well, I could give you my address and you could drop them off when you've finished with them. That is . . .' I took a breath. '. . . if you're here for some time and aren't about to whisk them back to

• *17* •

America or something!' (I gave a bit of a creepy fake laugh here but I prefer not to dwell on that bit.)

'Wow! That would be great. Maybe I could come round . . . you know, hang out . . .'

'Er . . . I'm quite busy . . .' I didn't want to be *too* mean if his brother was so ill, but on the other hand . . . 'I must get on,' I said backing away, because Gus was standing *much* too close now. 'You know, get those Robin Hood books . . .'

'I'll come with you,' he said firmly, gazing up at me. 'I love tall girls . . .'

I decided it was best to ignore this remark.

'No, don't you worry, you wait at the desk. I'll be quicker on my own,' I said, deciding to make a bolt for the History section, which is off to the far side of the library, and hide there.

I thought I had lost him when I heard a girl's voice calling out, 'Carrie?'

A moment later, Gus's head appeared round the end of the bookshelf, alerted to my presence, obviously delighted to find me again.

I turned, slightly irritated, towards the voice that had given away my position, and looked down to see Florence Graham blushing furiously. She always blushed easily – she has that clear, pale skin that goes with her beautiful deep red hair. She's just left Woodside Primary, and she's coming to Boughton High next term. I know her because her mum works part-time in the village shop and Moulton is a very, very, small place.

Last term, Florence was in the group I took around the school when they came to see what their secondary education fate was going to be. Rani was going to wear a T-shirt with *Run while you still can!* on it and mine was going to say *Abandon hope all ye who enter here* but they are not keen on humour in our school so we didn't. Rani had Donna and Shanaid in her group – which kind of clinched the avoidance of Miss Lamb's summer arts and drama course for both of us. Helping me show my group around was Simon Honeyman; with his blond hair and confident smile, I guessed he was the best-looking boy in our Year Seven last year. He certainly had all the girls in my group in a twitter. Except Florence, who hadn't said a word.

As we'd wandered down the corridor to the gym hall, Rani's group was coming down towards us. I could see Donna and Shanaid perking up no end at the sight of us approaching, and I knew why. But Simon was busy telling Florence about the football facilities (he's good-looking, but he *is* a Year Seven) and he didn't even look up as they got close. Desperate, Donna had called out loudly, 'Hey, Carrots! How's it going?' at Florence. She had now got everyone's attention. She then glanced down. '*Love* those shoes, by the way . . .'

Florence was wearing a pair of not-so-new trainers.

Florence immediately went scarlet and I zapped Donna with my iciest glare.

'What?' She stared at me, unphased, putting her hands up in the air. '*What?* I said I *loved* them, didn't I?'

And she and Shanaid continued down the corridor giggling, whilst Rani and I made low sideways snarling noises at each other as we passed.

And now, stuck in the History section of Middleton library, I felt bad because Florence wasn't looking that happy again, but this time it was my fault. I tried to ignore my new American pal, who was now standing at my side, and pulled myself together.

'Sorry, Florence, I was miles away. How are you? Hope you enjoyed the school visit. Looking forward to coming to Boughton next term?'

She bit her lip and didn't answer the question. She said instead, 'I didn't mean to interrupt you, I just wondered if you were, er, going to be helping out this year . . . You know, at Miss Lamb's arts and drama course? Your mum told mine that you might be.'

I remembered seeing her mum coming out of Mum's office at the end of term.

'Oh, no,' I sighed, shaking my head. 'Not this year. I'm afraid by the time I volunteered, Miss Lamb had all the helpers she needed.' I put on the regretful face I had used with Mum.

Florence's face fell. 'Oh, I see. I just wondered, that's all.'

'Won't your friends be there?' I asked.

She said nothing, and then blurted out, 'My best friend moved away a year ago. I didn't want to go at all, but Mum said I absolutely had to. She's got to work and she said I'd be bored at home on my own, but I *won't*. I'd *rather* be on my own.'

I gave her a big, encouraging smile. 'But it will be *great*, Florence, you'll have such a good time. There'll be other girls from your year there . . .' And then I caught her eye and I simply said, 'It'll be *great*,' again and tried to sound enthusiastic. 'Er . . . look, I've got to dash . . .'

Gus was almost, but not quite, *leaning* on me now. I was eager to get my pile of Robin Hood books stamped, just to get rid of him.

As we walked to the desk together, I suddenly heard a voice. A tall blonde woman was standing at the doorway. 'Gus, what are you *doing*? We've got to go, *now!*' And he shot off. Just like that. Leaving me holding a huge pile of books on Robin Hood.

Mrs Brigstock glared at me as she stamped them all. I know it was childish of me, but it was worth it to see her face curdle. I didn't know why Gus had suddenly had to dash like that. Maybe a medical emergency with his brother. If I took the books out I could at least be helpful if I saw him again.

The next thing that happened was typical of the way fate works constantly against me. But I have just heard the front door go. Mum is back. I have left the books in a heap in the hall. I will just go and shut my bedroom door.

## 5.00 p.m.

Right, where was I? Yes. Standing next to Florence. We had met up again waiting at the bus stop. I was fighting to get my umbrella to go the right way. It wouldn't, so I was beating it against the lamp post, partly in a rage and partly in frustration at life in general. I was in mid-smash when a car drew alongside me at the traffic lights and I glanced up at the back window to see Gus beaming back out at me. There appeared to be an older boy beside him, but I couldn't really tell, as whoever it was had his hat pulled low over his face and a pair of shades on, which I guessed must be something to do with his tragic illness.

Instantly, because I have the reflexes of a cheetah when I need to, I grabbed a book out of my plastic bag, lunged towards the car and tried to hold it up against the window. The elegant blonde woman who had called for Gus in the library turned round from the wheel, with a look of total horror on her face.

'Gus! Gus!' I shrieked. 'Look! I got you the books!' I shrieked, 'They're all in here!' I waved the bag around wildly with my free hand.

Several things then happened that I wasn't expecting.

1. Gus stopped grinning and turned away like he'd never seen me in his life.

2. The boy next to him pulled a mackintosh over his head and ducked down.

3. The lights changed and the woman shot off at top speed with a terrified expression on her face and a screech of tyres.

I turned to Florence. 'Well! What do make of that?' I gasped. 'You try and help people . . .'

'Did you know them?' she asked cautiously.

'Yes! No . . . I knew him. The boy. I mean, we'd only had one conversation, just now, in the library. Honestly, I was trying to do him a favour! And *that's* the thanks I get.'

'Mmm . . . None of them seemed, well, exactly *happy* to see you,' she offered tentatively.

'Thank you, Florence, I think I noticed that for myself.' I sniffed.

'No. Sorry. I didn't mean it to sound . . . I'm sure it was more like they were *frightened*, er, no – *surprised* by you.'

I wasn't sure if that made me feel better or not, but the bus came and we clambered on. 'I guess maybe they want to keep his illness private or something,' I sighed, sitting down and trying to find a place for the disobedient umbrella, but they don't have bins on buses. 'Weird, though – that boy was *desperate* to be friends in the library.'

'You've got plenty of friends, Carrie.' Florence was sitting next to me, staring with her intense grey eyes. 'Everyone likes you . . . you just *get on* with people.'

'Mmm . . .' I said, thinking of Jet. 'Not *every*one. And let's face it, what just happened wasn't the most *popular* experience I've ever had in my life.'

'Sometimes popular girls aren't necessarily the nicest ones,' Florence said thoughtfully.

I looked hard at her. 'Don't confuse the girl that everyone's scared of with the girl everyone likes, Florence. It's not the same.'

'It is in our year.' She sighed and turned to look out of the window.

Which just goes to show that life can be hard at any age.

And I understood exactly why she wasn't too keen on the arts and drama course.

*And* if I ever see that boy Gus again he will get a piece of my mind. Making me put up with all that dreadful flirting, making me feel sorry for him and getting me to help him, and then doing a disappearing act. I mean, what was that all about?

All most confusing.

Hmm . . . Mum is yelling something up the stairs about Robin Hood. She sounds pretty mad. Better go.

**CHLOE'S TIP:** • • • • • • • • • • • • • • • • • • • •

*Miserable weather doesn't have to mean frumpy wellies, tent-like overcoats and depressing black wind-broken umbrellas. Colourful, well-fitting and comfortable clothes that keep you warm and dry can really help brighten your mood. Try a tailored coat in your favourite colour, a cosy knit scarf and matching beanie, cute wellies, and a good quality umbrella with a print that makes you smile.*

# Chapter 4

Thursday 11.00 a.m.

Rani is back tomorrow! I will no longer be friendless and alone in the world. She is coming round first thing in the morning which is good, good, good, as I am officially hysterical.

However, when I tell her my news *she* will be officially hysterical too.

And so no help to anyone.

My life is about to be turned upside down.

The Cat in the Hat has arrived!

Well, not literally, but something has happened equally as amazing and a lot more exciting.

But I must start at the beginning, as Dr Jennings will need all the details for my future therapy sessions. There is no doubt at all in my mind that this will be one of the most significant events in my life.

For once it wasn't raining, and I was helping Mum and Dad clean up what they like to call garden furniture, and I like to call an odd assortment of old tables and chairs, for their barbecue party on Saturday when Ned came out and said Maddy's mum was on the phone.

Mum then disappeared for ages. I thought she was making the call last extra long to skive off garden duties but when she came back out again she was all bright-eyed and excited-looking, and her hair had a wilder frizz about it than usual.

'Seems like we've got some extra guests for our party on Saturday,' she said, beaming. Dad nodded for me to put down the table we were carrying.

'Who's that, then?' he asked.

'Yes, who?' I echoed, purely out of politeness.

'We-ell. Maddy's father met up with a friend just after we left California. A friend who needed a place for his wife and two children to stay in England for a while, and, as the Van de Veldes are staying on at their Malibu house, he's offered them their house here, so they're living in it. He thought it would be nice for them to meet some of their friends and when I suggested inviting them to our barbecue party he thought it was a great idea. So I called them just now and they're coming! Just think, Carrie, real Americans. You'll feel right at home . . . and that's not the most exciting part!'

But I knew where this was going. It had to be. It was destiny.

'Stop right there, Mum!' I yelped. 'Don't tell me, they have a son.'

Mum looked confused. 'Well, yes.'

'I've met him already.'

Mum started back. 'What on earth are you talking about? You *can't* have met him already.'

'I promise you, I have.'

'Well, I'm *amazed* you kept that to yourself. I would have thought it would have been your dream come true.'

'*Dream come true!* Hardly,' I snorted.

Mum's eyes were popping out of her head and she flopped backwards into a wicker chair. 'Well, I'm staggered,' she gasped, staring at me. 'Absolutely stunned. I thought you'd be *thrilled*.'

'Thrilled! Why on earth would you think that? I *tried* to be nice to the odious little twerp. I met him in the library and offered to help him out with some books – yes, the Robin Hood ones – because of the terminal illness in the family, but when I saw him in his car outside he was all weird and the rest of them blanked me and they drove off at a hundred miles an hour. Like I had the plague or leprosy or something.' I indicated to Dad I was ready to pick up the table again. 'Well, you can invite them if you must, but I'm warning you, they will all be getting the cold shoulder from *me*, the bunch of ungrateful nutters!'

Mum was speechless for a moment, then said slowly, 'About the car thing, I think they must have thought you were a fan. And you were drawing attention to their car.'

'A fan? A *fan*! Don't make me laugh. Of that tiny toad? I've never heard of him! Nobody's heard of him. *Gus*. How can I be a *fan*?'

Mum began to smile again. 'Not of *him*. Of his *brother*.'

'His brother? You mean Mr Mackintosh Over His Head? The dying one?'

Mum took a deep breath. 'Yes. And he is *not* dying by the way, I don't know where you got that from. His brother. Mr Mackintosh – *what* did you call him?'

'Doesn't matter,' I sighed. 'Who is he, then?'

She put her head on one side. 'We-ell, in your opinion he's the best-looking, most talented actor in the whole —'

I put the table back down again. 'Stop right there, Mum. Do you actually mean in *my* opinion? Or are you about to say someone really lame that *you* like, like from your sad doctor telly series?'

Mum shook her head. 'No, he's definitely *your* favourite. In fact, I would say that you've actually had a major crush on this person for some time. You certainly watch the TV series he's in often enough.'

'No! Not . . .' I felt a dizziness come upon me. But this was Mum talking. She was bound to have got it wrong. I didn't dare hope . . . 'Is he in *Hollywood High*?' I asked flatly. Just to get it over with. I braced myself for inevitable disappointment.

'*Was*. Was mysteriously not in the series Ned just filmed. Which is connected to why he's here now.'

'Is it —? Oh my God! It *can't* be!' I screamed.

Mum nodded, grinning from ear to ear. 'The very same . . .'

My mind was racing, going back to the figure in the car, before he pulled the coat over . . . Could it have been, could it *really* have been . . .?

'Noooooo!' I howled. 'No! It can't be! OH MY GOD!' And I had to run around the garden screeching a couple of times before I was calm enough to say, 'But *why*? What on earth is Gregg Madison doing here? And is he really not dying?'

'He's got the part in an American film about the young Robin Hood, and they're filming most of it in Bracken Forest. His mother didn't want a hotel, because it's not private enough, and the paparazzi can wander in and out, so the Van de Veldes' house was perfect. It's gated and you can't see the house from the road. They've had to be very hush hush as the deal wasn't signed and sealed until yesterday. So there you go! We're going to be nearly neighbours! And no, he's not dying, he's absolutely well in every possible way.'

But my mind was racing again. The Van de Veldes' house *is* perfect for a Hollywood star. It is architect-designed, huge, airy and white with floor-to-ceiling glass and bleached-wood floors and a pool and massive limestone bathrooms with thousands of spotless white towels.

Not like our house. Which is in a boring, quiet street of other houses that look just the same, with rugs that are a bit worn, and a sofa that has needed recovering since the nail-varnish incident, and a skateboard in the downstairs loo which Ned keeps there along with a selection of skateboarding magazines. And then there's my old school photograph propped up on the kitchen dresser, the one that Ned drew the black eyebrows on. I began to hyperventilate.

So I have come up to my room to be hysterical on many levels and wait for Rani to arrive tomorrow.

And try to remember to breathe.

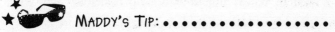 MADDY'S TIP: •••••••••••••••••••
One of the easiest ways to breathe new life into a room
is to decorate it with pictures that mean something to
people who use it. Use inexpensive photo frames, or use
mini-pegs to hang up photos like laundry across a wall.
You can always get your pictures put on fabrics or make
a collage. Get creative!

# *Chapter 5*

I am exhausted.

Thank goodness Rani is back.

After shrieking at each other for half an hour this morning about Gregg Madison, she made us go upstairs and lie in a darkened room with wet face cloths over our foreheads to try and calm ourselves down. She took the duvet off my bed and laid it on the carpet, then lay down on it with her hands on her chest as if in prayer.

'Take a really deep breath,' her voice said from the floor, 'and let's say to ourselves, "We are composed".'

'We are composed,' I echoed from my bed.

'Just because an incredibly famous TV star is coming to this very house tomorrow . . .'

I tried to repeat it, but Rani said my voice had gone too squeaky and instead she told me to repeat, 'We are *not* silly star-struck girls.'

'We are *not* silly star-struck girls.'

'We are mature women of the world.'

'We are mature women of the world.'

'He's just a boy.'

'He's just a —'

'Going too squeaky again, Carrie.'

'Sorry.'

She continued. 'We are going to be dead cool about this so when we tell everyone else – especially Jet – it will seem like it wasn't a big deal to us at all . . .'

'What! Rani! That's too long! But I agree. We'll just say to them, "Oh yes, Gregg Madison came round. Have you met him? He's *sooo* nice. I suppose you could say we're good friends now".' I began to let my imagination run away with me here . . . '"Oh look, that's my phone going off, Jet, there's a text from him. Honestly, he never stops texting me now – I think it's because we definitely discovered that we shared a special bond . . ."'

'Hmm, hmm. Carrie!' A warning voice rose from the floor.

'Sorry, Rani. Did I get carried away?'

'Yes.'

I rolled over and stared down over the edge of my bed at her. 'It might happen. He might really like us and we could hang out together for the rest of the holidays.'

'Won't he be away filming and stuff?'

'Filming won't start straight away, surely. Can we practise how we're going to say hello?' I lay back down.

'Not again! I want to talk about how I didn't meet a single boy I liked on holiday and that's just not fair because I've never even had a proper boyfriend *here*, unlike *some* people.'

'Please?'

I heard a groan.

'Can we talk about my lack-of-boyfriend situation afterwards, then?'

'Yes. Promise. And then will you tell me what you think of my idea to decorate the garden so it doesn't look too horrible? Oh my God! Gregg Madison might be using our loo!'

'Don't tell me, you'll never use it again? You will turn it into a shrine and you will come and worship at the sacred toilet bowl.'

'Yuck! Gross.' I chucked my pillow down on her.

Rani, who is nothing if not organised, sat up, like a mummy from the tomb. 'This needs planning, Carrie. We've got a lot to get through. We can talk about my lack-of-boyfriend situation while we work.'

## 11.00 p.m.

Mum just came in and said we should get a good night's sleep and to turn my light out. Sleep! What a joke. Luckily I have my trusty torch.

Before Rani could even write *Number 1* on her Things to Do list, we were interrupted by my phone. For one mad minute I actually thought it might be Gregg, but it was Jack. Calling on a terrible line from Thailand. He is coming back on Monday. It is a week early! His mum is having retail therapy withdrawal and wants to head back to her Paris apartment. Jack is coming home to his dad at Pitsford Hall, or the Pitsford Palace as Rani calls it.

'Isn't that brilliant?' he said.

It was a terrible phone connection.

'Brilliant! Guess what?' I shrieked down the line. 'Guess who's coming to our house tomorrow?'

'Madonna?

'*No!*'

'The Queen?'

'Duh. No.'

'Michael Jackson?'

'No! Guess again.'

'I don't want to be a killjoy, Carrie, but this game could go on for quite some time and this call is costing a fortune. I don't *know*! Who?'

'Gregg Madison!'

'Who?'

'Gregg Madison! You know who he is, from *Hollywood High* . . . the series Ned got the part in.'

'Which one is he? Is he the short fat one with the potato face?'

'No! The blond one, the good-looking lead who left.'

'Oh, right, the one with two expressions – wistful, and concerned in a where-did-I-put-my-pen-type way.'

'Stop it, Jack! He's brilliant.'

'Brilliant? Mmm, I'll give you he's pretty good. But I don't get it, how come you're going to meet him?'

'Maddy's dad knows his dad, they're staying at Maddy's *house*. He's got the lead in a young Robin Hood film and they're shooting it in Bracken Forest. Isn't that amazing?'

'Amazing.' There was a pause. 'How long is he staying?'

'Quite a while, I think. Maybe you'll get to meet him too when you get back, if all goes well tomorrow at the party and he likes us. Won't that be cool?'

'Oooh, cool. I can hardly wait.'

And then the line went too fizzy and his voice disappeared.

And Rani was looking at me in a Rani-type way.

'What?' I asked.

'Nothing.'

'Don't nothing me. What?'

'How was Jack?'

'He was fine. Well, I didn't really have time to ask too much about what he was up to . . .'

Rani pursed her lips in that way she does. 'Mmm . . . So I noticed.'

'Look, Rani, Jack was fine, and anyway when he's back he can tell me all about his holiday, OK? Come on, tomorrow Chloe will be back. We're nearly all together again. It's going to be brilliant. When Jack returns he'll be thrilled to get to meet a real-life TV star. The gang all together again *and* Gregg Madison, what more could you ask for?'

'Oh yes, a real-life TV star. Who you have a big crush on. I bet Jack can hardly wait.'

'Don't say it like that, Rani. I appreciate Gregg's talent and good looks purely from an intellectual point of view.' Rani snorted, so I went on. 'Come on, I know you're excited too! How often do we get to meet a real-life famous person?'

Rani's serious face vanished and she couldn't help grinning. 'I know! And we haven't even started on what we're going to wear . . .'

'I know at least one thing that I'm going to wear . . .'

'Not the horrible lucky Union Jack knickers?'

'Yup.'

**CARRIE'S TIP:** • • • • • • • • • • • • • • • • • •

It's tempting to put too much effort into your appearance when you want to make a good impression, but try not to get carried away. Asking for a friend's opinion beforehand can avoid you looking like a celebrity from the 'What Were They Thinking?' pages. More importantly, if your shoes are giving you blisters, your top's too tight and you have to keep sweeping your hair from your eyes, it attracts the wrong sort of attention and it's not attractive, no matter how good you thought you looked doing your model poses in the bedroom mirror!

# *Chapter 6*

*Saturday 7.00 p.m.*

OK. Today I met someone who I have *admired* for a long time. I am feeling slightly confused and dizzy about it all.

The one thing I have to say before I write anything else is that I do, do, do *NOT* have a crush on Gregg Madison.

Crushes are just so immature and anyway you have them on people like film stars and singers who you don't know. I *know* Gregg Madison now. So that makes it totally different. I *know* his personality after a whole afternoon in his company. And it is fantastic.

And I really don't want to be big-headed or anything, but he really did seem to like me too. Even though he knows I have a boyfriend.

He was so nice and not stuck-up or starry at all, but asked me loads of questions about my life and friends, and said he just couldn't get enough of English accents . . . but I am getting ahead of myself.

The day started early when Rani's mum dropped off some tablecloths and cushions. I had decided on an old-fashioned-English-tea-in-the-garden theme. Tom came over as well to help us achieve my vision. Mum was bemused when I asked her if we could decorate the garden, but this was to be expected. She has no taste. She has special needs in the taste department. You only have to look at her clothes. She should be given a badge to pin on to her outfits to explain.

It does mean, however, that she doesn't mind when you say things like 'Can we decorate the garden?' because she is incapable of an opinion about such matters so she doesn't care what you do. I could have carefully covered every table in black bin liners and rested a bunch of bananas on a nest of hay in the middle and she'd still have gone, 'That's nice, dear.'

Instead, I borrowed some faded floral and patchwork tablecloths from Rani's mum and draped them over the assortment of tables dotted about the garden. Then we filled some chipped cream jugs I found in the shed with roses from our bushes and put a jug spilling over with the sweetly scented pink and white flowers on each table. Finally, Tom brought some pastel-coloured bunting that his mum used at Moulton Fair and we hung it from tree to tree.

After strategically rearranging some of the large pots of flowers and several wicker chairs with cushions, we stood back and surveyed our handiwork.

'It looks really pretty,' Rani pronounced.

'It does, doesn't it?' I agreed.

'Very English tea party,' Rani said, nodding. 'Like in those old films.'

'Exactly the look I wanted.' I beamed. And then I spotted Dad coming out of the back door brandishing cooking utensils in his barbecue apron – the red one with the bra and pants on the front.

Quite honestly, I despair.

I moved forward to protest, but Rani grabbed me and said we

didn't have time and dragged me upstairs to get ready.

After ten clothes changes, I opted for denim shorts (legs still just brown enough) and a pink strappy top. Rani experimented with my hair by plaiting it and curling the plaits up by my ears but I decided it was too Princess Leia from *Star Wars* and just wore it loose. Rani plaited hers but as her hair is dark she avoids the Heidi-Goes-Mental look I get with mine. She wore a black cotton shift dress and black strappy sandals with very high heels which were only going to get stuck in the lawn but she is always a girl to sacrifice comfort for style, and she is very small. I chose pink flip flops, as I am not.

Rani and I then spent quite a lot of time arranging ourselves in different places in the garden to look our best, and deciding which sitting position made our thighs looked thinnest, so we would be absolutely ready when Gregg arrived. However, because-fate-is-so-often-against-me, Gregg, Gus and the elegant blonde woman appeared with Mum at the precise moment Dad had just called me over and thrust a plate of uncooked sausages in my hands. Dad turned to welcome his guests and in a panic I chucked the sausages straight into the hedge. I am sorry, but I will not meet my idol with a plate of raw pork clasped to my bosom.

Walking next to the elegant blonde, who was now obviously Mrs Madison, was a short, sharp-eyed woman with close-cropped dark hair, talking urgently into her mobile. She barely glanced around the garden. Behind her, Gus was beaming at me without a trace of embarrassment at the humongous lie he'd told me, and next to Gus was HIM.

All practice 'hellos' went out of my head. I swallowed hard. Tall (hooray!), tanned and impossibly handsome, like his mother he was smiling at everyone, and not with a horrible lecherous face like his revolting younger brother. Mum beamed at me and started to bring them over.

Rani hissed, 'We are not silly star-struck girls . . .' over and over as they approached.

I regretted the shorts immediately, as I suspected everyone could see my legs wobble, and then he was *there*, right in front of us, in dark blue jeans and a ridiculously cool faded green T-shirt.

'I'd like to introduce you to Carrie and Rani, Maddy's great friends,' Mum said, beaming.

Gus jumped in first. 'It's my library girl! Fantastic to see you again!'

'Hello, Gus,' I responded calmly. I wasn't going to forgive and forget *that* easily. 'Sorry I scared your mother and brother in the car. But I got those books out for you, you know, just in case we met again. You know, the ones for your *incredibly sick* brother . . .'

Gus giggled. 'Sorry I lied, but we'd all been sworn to secrecy till now. You can give them to Gregg – they were for him, as you've probably guessed by now.'

'What's this about?' Gregg asked, and then he looked at me, frowned, and broke into a grin. 'Hey, aren't you the umbrella girl?'

I nodded dumbly. This wasn't going quite as I had imagined.

'Mom said she thought you must have recognised me when you, er . . . came up to the car. She said I didn't have the hat pulled far enough down.'

Mrs Madison looked deeply embarrassed. 'I'm so sorry, Carrie, honey, but we have to be careful. Some fans are so . . . well . . . and you did kind of *rush* at the car . . . Anyway, we were still very much trying to keep a low profile. However, now Gregg's signed the deal, it doesn't have to be such a secret we're here. I mean, we obviously had *no* idea that you were a friend of Maddy's, and Gus did explain his awful lie. So sorry about that as well.'

'But you came through, Carrie!' And Gus *winked* at me. Again.

'I didn't recognise you at all, Gregg . . .' I babbled, still hypnotised by his blue eyes, which were looking directly at *me*! 'I don't know how I didn't, I've watched every episode of *Hollywood High* like a million times, I should be able to recognise you in the dark by now . . .'

I stopped because Rani was treading slowly but forcefully on my foot. I took the hint and stopped talking.

'Hi, I'm Rani,' she said calmly, like he was just someone from school we'd met in the Coffee Bean. *Just* like we practised. 'I expect Maddy and Chloe told you loads about me . . .'

Which was *not* what we'd practised.

Gregg laughed. 'Well, I think you *were* mentioned once or twice.'

Rani shrieked. 'Oh my God! You really mean that. You *did* meet them!'

'Sure.' Gregg looked bemused. 'We hung out with them for about a week. I think we arrived in LA the day after you left.'

Fate. Against me. Again. Etc.

'And they didn't tell us?!' I gasped, moving away from Gus, who was *breathing* on my arm.

Mrs Madison stepped in. 'In their defence, I did tell Maddy and Chloe not to say anything about Gregg coming to England, not before the deal was signed. Maddy's father didn't even tell them we were going to use their house. I'm sure they spoke about *you* a lot though . . .'

'Chloe and Maddy certainly never mentioned either of you to *me*,' Gus said slyly. 'Two such great-looking girls . . . I'm surprised they kept *you* a secret . . .'

Mum cleared her throat. 'Why don't you young ones all sit down?' She indicated the table under the tree at the bottom of the garden. 'Now you must come with me.' She took Mrs Madison, who was looking at Gus with an exasperated expression, by the arm. 'I must introduce you to our new neighbours, Mr and Mrs Banks . . .'

Did Mum actually say, 'young ones'? She is determined to destroy me socially.

Rani and I took Gus and Gregg to sit down in the shade and, even though I gave Ned a massive warning glare, he not only came too but grabbed the seat next to Gregg. I would have fought him for it but knew somehow that this would lack dignity. Of course I got Mr Hot Breath next to me. Ned then plunged into a long conversation with Gregg about *all* the actors on *Hollywood High* and would have monopolised him forever if Ned and Gus hadn't thankfully been distracted by our neighbours' dogs having a massive fight over something in the hedge and felt compelled to get up and join the gathering crowd. Thank goodness some things are irresistible to younger boys.

I immediately moved into the vacated seat.

'Did you say you got some Robin Hood books out?' Gregg's blue eyes turned to me and he gave me a warm smile.

I had to resist the urge to run my hands all over his face, like a blind person, to check that he was real. Instead I said, 'Yes, I'll get them for you before you go.' Then I blurted out, 'I can't believe you're not in the new series of *Hollywood High*. You were amazing in the latest one. It just won't be the same without you.'

How cringe-making was that? That wasn't a bit like what I had rehearsed in my head, which was something funny and cool that I couldn't remember a word of.

'It was time to move on,' Gregg replied. 'Let's hope you like me as much in *Robin Hood*.'

'Oh, I know I will . . .' I gushed and Rani trod on my foot again.

Then Tom came over. Ever since he had arrived, Dad had had him on barbecue and dog-handling duty, and I introduced him. Me! Introducing someone to Gregg Madison. Tom sank his large, stocky frame into an empty chair, pushed a thatch of dark hair off his forehead and poured himself a massive glass of Mum's homemade lemonade. I noticed Gregg staring at him intently. I think actors are so naturally *interested* in people, aren't they?

'Gregg,' I said, smiling, 'I'm sure if you've met Chloe you know all about Tom. He's been her boyfriend forever.' I looked at my watch. 'Where is she? She's supposed to be coming straight from the airport. Her mum's bringing her – they should have been here a while ago.'

'Chloe's coming *here*? This afternoon?' Gregg sounded shocked.

'Yes. You must be *so* excited about seeing her again.'

Gregg looked at me strangely.

'Not you!' I laughed, realising his mistake. 'I was talking to Tom!'

Tom grinned. 'Sure am. Feels like ages.' He raised a tall pink glass. (After my nagging and an emergency trip into town Mum had produced some green plates and pink glasses that matched the faded floral prints on the tablecloths.) 'To the return of Chloe,' he cried.

Then suddenly his face lit up at the sight of something over my shoulder, and I knew that she had arrived.

We all turned to watch her make her way across the sunlit garden.

As always, Chloe made every girl there wish they looked as good as her. She had tied back the dark curls from her pretty face with a green ribbon which matched her eyes. She was wearing a pink and white floral print dress which looked great against her Californian tan, and on her feet she had plain white pumps. I noticed as she got nearer that her nose had got a dusting of tiny pinprick dark freckles. Rani, Tom and I leapt up and fell on Chloe with cries of welcome. When I had managed to pull Tom off her I dragged her to the table.

'Guess who's here?' I asked her.

'Hi, Chloe. Bet you didn't expect to see us again so soon.'

That Gregg really does *stare* sometimes.

Chloe looked shocked. 'Gregg?' she gasped. 'What are you doing here? I mean, I knew you were talking about a role that involved filming in England, but I wasn't expecting you to pop up in Carrie's garden!'

'It was kind of hush-hush. My dad arranged staying here at the last minute with Mr Van de Velde. We wanted somewhere quiet to hang out for a while before filming started. A hotel is way too public.'

He brushed his hair off his face, and went on. 'Anyway, Carrie's mom knows the Van de Veldes and invited us over, so here we are. Enjoying this lovely English garden on a summer afternoon. Weird to think we were on the beach in LA only a week ago, isn't it?'

Chloe appeared to be momentarily lost for words, and I could appreciate why. It was a lot to take in. You might expect to meet a TV star at Maddy's Malibu beach house (not that *I* did because fate is so often against me), but you don't expect to step off the plane and find one in my garden. Tom came up and put his arm around her. 'Isn't this brilliant? I'm glad you had a great time, but I'm glad you're back home at last.' Chloe must have been jet-lagged because she didn't really respond, and we were feeling a tiny bit uncomfortable in the pause afterwards when Miss Lamb descended on us like a train at full steam.

'Carrie! Rani! Chloe!' She heaved up alongside us. 'MARVELLOUS. You're all back. What a piece of luck.'

Everyone knows it is disconcerting to meet teachers out of school, but with Mum's job I have had to get used to it. To be fair, Miss Lamb was the only teacher invited today. She is a woman of impressive stature with a love of flowing, dramatic lines in her garments. Her necklace didn't so much have stones as boulders roped together, *à la* Stone Age. Hanging down her back was a long, grey plait, like a Native American's. This is not cool on an English woman of advancing years. On her wide feet she had abandoned her usual leather lace-up shoes and was in sandals, thick of sole and broad of strap. Miss Lamb has never married. She has devoted herself to the arts.

'I've just spoken to your mother. She says you might have some free time on your hands . . .'

She had to be kidding! Not *now*. Not now some glamour and excitement had entered my life.

'And now Rani and Chloe are back as well. I have to tell you I am DESPERATE for help for this year's arts and drama course. DESPERATE.'

'But, but . . . I thought you had plenty of help,' Rani said nervously.

'NO! Three of my volunteers have just had to pull out. It's a TRAGEDY, I tell you, a total DISASTER. This year's *Cinderella* is hanging in the balance . . .'

By now everyone in the garden and probably the street knew that that there was something very amiss in Miss Lamb's life. People around the garden were *looking on*. I looked at Rani in panic. 'Erm, actually we've got quite a lot on at the moment . . .'

'Oh dear. Really? It's just that the children enjoy it so. Of course, it will still be POSSIBLE without extra hands, but . . .' Miss Lamb suddenly looked uncharacteristically defeated and tired. 'I had hoped that this year we could really show that dreadful Mrs Jackson who organises the Pitsford Fête that we could put on a show to rival theirs, she does like to crow so. Never mind, it will be just rather more work than I anticipated, that's all . . .' She tailed off.

Rani and I looked at each other.

We liked Miss Lamb. She was a good drama teacher, and we knew how hard she worked in the holidays with children in the area. I also couldn't help thinking about Florence. But what about our new glamorous friends?

'We-ell . . .' I began. Hope lit up Miss Lamb's eyes.

'I'll help!'

Surprised, we all spun round to stare at Chloe. Surely she would be wanting to spend every moment with Tom now she was back. He was staring at her, obviously as confused as we were.

'OH, THANK YOU.' Miss Lamb beamed at her. 'I know how clever you are with clothes. You can do costumes . . .' Her eyes glided back to Rani and me. 'And I know how good you are with hair and make-up, Rani, and Carrie is so good at design, which would be *such* a help with scenery . . .'

Rani looked at me and I looked at her and we resigned ourselves to our fate.

'OK. We'll do it,' we said together.

Miss Lamb clapped her hands. 'WONDERFUL! Simply terrific news. We need all the help we can get.'

'Would you like one more?'

My eyes nearly popped out of my head. It was Gregg. Was a Hollywood TV star really volunteering to help out at Miss Lamb's arts and drama course? I wasn't the only one who was surprised. I heard Chloe gasp too.

'I could spare a couple of mornings . . .' Gregg went on.

'Me too!' yelled Gus.

'No way!' Gregg laughed. 'You're too young. And anyway, you know your dad's in London for a while, and you're going down to see him.'

*Your dad.* So they had different dads. *That* explained a lot.

'Well, Gregg, that would be *wonderful*!' Miss Lamb spluttered.

'You could help with auditions. Imagine!' She put her hand on her ample chest as if to calm her beating heart. Talk about her lucky day.

'Volunteering for something, Gregg?' a sharp voice said. It was the hard-faced woman who had arrived with them. I had noticed her keeping an eye on our table earlier.

'Everyone, this is my publicity agent Mona Laverne,' Gregg said. Mona shot an icicle smile around the table. Gregg wrinkled his perfect, tanned nose. 'I could help out a few times, couldn't I?' he said pleadingly. 'I've got some time before shooting starts.'

Mum had appeared at the end of this exchange with a refill for the jug of homemade lemonade and leapt in.

'Moulton Fair is a very English event, I can assure you. Very traditional, with stalls and entertainment, bunting, that sort of thing. It's a wonderful experience for any visitor to the area.'

Which I must say is a bit of an exaggeration, as it's barely more than a few tents in a field, but I wasn't going to contradict her.

'Bunting?' Mona frowned.

Mum pointed at the rows of little pretty cotton triangles strung up across the garden – hundreds of pink, blue and pale green flags fluttering in the breeze.

Mona looked thoughtful. 'Hmm . . . Helping out local kids . . . Village fair . . . Actually, it could all be good. That's not a bad idea. Nice visual. Could be a nice English-feel story.' She smiled at Gregg. 'Sure, a couple of mornings . . . Why not?'

Mum turned to wink at me as she and Mona drifted off back up the garden again.

There was a weird silence after that. Gus was looking annoyed,

Gregg was grinning broadly, Chloe and Tom were both looking confused and Rani and I were looking both confused *and* delighted.

'*Why* did he say he'd do it?' Rani asked after I had handed over my Robin Hood books to Gregg and they'd gone. At last we were alone in my room.

I was pretty sure I knew the answer to that question.

I don't want to be big-headed, but he had made the most massive effort to be super nice to me today. I *know* it wasn't my imagination.

I think he really likes *me*. ME! Carrie Henderson of Moulton village.

However I told Rani that I didn't know why.

Rani grinned. 'God, Carrie, you do have a bit of a crush on him, don't you? What about Jack?'

'Don't be silly,' I replied. 'Of course I haven't got a crush on him. He's just a really, really nice genuine person, isn't he?'

Rani sighed. 'Actually, I think he is.'

So I'm feeling rather confused and excited and weird all at the same time. As if Gregg Madison is a big spoon that's going to stir us all up.

 RANI'S TIP: •••••••••••••••••••••

The fool-proof look for a summer party or barbecue is a
fresh-faced natural one. Apply a little tinted moisturiser if you
need foundation, or some pressed powder if you get a shiny
T-zone. Add a little bronzed blusher for a summer glow and
choose a light, natural shade of lip-gloss and you're good to go!

# Chapter 7

## Sunday 9.30 p.m.

Too exhausted to write anything. For once Mum is right. The excitement has been too much for me.

## Monday 8.00 a.m.

I am still feeling mixed-up. It may be lack of sleep, of course. When is a crush not a crush, but the real thing? The basis of a real relationship? Rani says that Gus has a crush on me, but in that case it's just annoying. But don't all relationships start with crush-like feelings? And how can you tell the difference?

I know I'm crazy about Jack, so what's going on? I keep trying to remember what kissing Jack is like, and Gregg's head keeps getting in the way.

And Jack is coming back today. We are meeting at the Coffee Bean after I've finished at Miss Lamb's. What if I kiss him and Gregg's head won't go away?

What would it be like dating a superstar-famous TV actor?

I have been up doing my hair and make-up so it looks like I'm not really trying too hard. This has taken ages and ages. It is all because Jack, *my boyfriend*, is coming back today. It really is.

My boyfriend who I do, do, do adore. Really.

But first I have to spend the morning with Gregg. Who, I

cannot deny, is showing more than a passing interest in me. It's all very disturbing.

First life was too boring and now there's too much going on.

I may even be too excited to eat breakfast.

## 9.00 a.m.

Trust Mum to bring me back down to earth. I was just managing to get down a few small slices of toast when she announced that she has volunteered me to take the new neighbour's daughter to Miss Lamb's arts and drama course at the village hall.

'I said you'd be happy to, Carrie. She won't know a soul. They were thrilled when I told them about it yesterday at the party, and Miss Lamb said she'd be welcome. It's a great opportunity for her to meet other girls in the area, especially as she's coming to Boughton High in September. She only got back fom visiting her gran yesterday. That's why her parents couldn't stay very long – they were picking her up from the airport.'

'*Mum!*'

'I said you'd ring the bell and pick her up on your way.'

'*Mum!*'

'I'm sure you can remember being her age and being anxious and shy . . .'

'*Mum!*'

That is all you can say, really. Resistance is useless. How mums feel they can offer your services to the community without consulting you I do not know. My human rights have been violated.

I had better go and get her, then.

\* \* \*

## 7.00 p.m.

I have now met Miss Talullah Banks.

I pressed the bell and Mrs Banks answered. I had already noticed at the barbecue that Mrs Banks is always beautifully dressed, and looking at her standing at the door this morning in her shiny red kitten heels, pretty red and black flowery skirt and a stylish red wrapover top, I could only hope that she might pass on some fashion tips to Mum.

Mum had told me that Mrs Banks' family are originally from Jamaica and with her huge dark eyes, glowing brown skin and amazing smile, I thought she looked like a film star, then Mr Banks appeared and said hello. I was disappointed with Mr Banks. Mr Banks does not look like a film star. Mr Banks looks like my dad. How Mr Banks ever got someone as stunning as Mrs Banks to marry him is a mystery to me.

'Talullah!' Mrs Banks called. 'Carrie's here!'

I put my head on one side in my kind, caring, 'Don't be shy, I'm here to look after you' way.

A girl appeared at the top of the stairs.

'Hi!' she cried, not taking her eyes off me as she bounded down. 'You're tall. And pretty. And I love your hair.'

'And, er, I . . . I love yours,' was all I managed to say in return.

And I did. Talullah Banks certainly made an impact. She was medium height, stocky and wearing long pink shorts with a bright yellow T-shirt. Her dark brown eyes sparkled in a pretty face that was now giving me an enormous smile. But the first thing you noticed about Talullah Banks was her hair – a glorious mass of tiny black spirals and corkscrews going off in every direction.

She patted it happily. 'It is gorgeous, isn't it?'

'Talullah!' her mother tutted.

'It is,' I laughed.

'Come on, then.' Talullah took my arm as if we'd known each other for years. 'Let's go to this arts and drama thing, then. You'll have to fill me in on what the other girls are like on the way . . . I want to know everything, especially who is nice and who is mean.'

I remembered what Mum had said. *'Anxious and shy . . .'*

Ha! Look out Donna and Shanaid.

Before we set off, Talullah felt compelled to climb the massive oak tree in their front garden. She went up and down like a cat.

'I like climbing that tree,' she said, dusting herself down. 'So, where were you?'

Rani joined us as we walked down the sunny tree-lined lane that led to the village hall and I introduced them.

'Aren't you lucky to have big boobs?' Talullah sighed at her.

Rani shot me a startled look. I simply shrugged, grinning to myself.

'I'm longing for mine to grow more, but there's just *no* movement at all in that department.' She peered down her T-shirt and made a sad tut-tutting noise. 'No movement at all.'

It is not often Rani is lost for words.

'So, tell me then, what's the deal with this arts and drama course?'

I decided to keep my description neutral. Talullah needed to make her own mind up about people.

When we walked in, Chloe was there already, standing in the middle of a crowd of children who were all milling about and shrieking, 'No, *you're* bound to be Cinderella!', 'No, *you* are!' at each other.

I noticed Donna was shrieking loudest and with the least conviction in her voice. It was quite obvious she thought the role was hers.

No sign of Gregg Madison. Miss Lamb obviously hadn't told the children, as they were only *very excited* – but not hysterical. It was going to be some surprise. I noticed Donna and Shanaid spotting Talullah and nudging each other. No doubt checking out their next victim. Although Talullah appeared to be a girl who could look after herself, I made a mental note to keep an eye on the situation. Miss Lamb then gathered all the Year Sixes together in one group. There were ten of them so far: Talullah, Donna and Shanaid and their little gang of Emma, April, Prema and Nicki, and Jeremy and two mad riding girls called Helena and Lily who think they are ponies and cycle round with reins on the handlebars of their bikes, neighing.

'Where's Florence?' Miss Lamb asked, checking her list.

And then she appeared at the door, looking pale and nervous.

'Hi Florence!' I called out. 'I came after all.' A look of relief crossed her face when she saw me. 'Come and meet Talullah, she's new and doesn't know anyone.'

Talullah was staring and staring at Florence. 'Wow, Florence!' she cried. 'Great hair!'

Miss Lamb then took Rani, Chloe and me behind the little stage and introduced us to Mr Hopper. Mr Hopper is Woodside Primary's new janitor. He is short and stocky with a droopy greying moustache, and kind-looking but with sad eyes. I think

Mum told me that his wife died a year or so ago. He showed Rani and me where the scenery was stored. Miss Lamb then led Chloe out to a large wardrobe full of clothes in the dressing room.

We began hauling out castle battlements, trees, and an enormous round moon which I immediately knew was going to be the basis of my pumpkin coach.

'I'm lovin' that Talullah.' Rani grinned, then she looked cautiously around her. 'I wanted to ask you something. Did you notice that Chloe has been in a really weird mood?'

'She's just acclimatising to being back here after California. It took me a while, I can tell you.'

'But she was so quiet at the barbecue, wasn't she? You must have noticed she hardly said a word.'

'I *did* a *bit*,' I said. 'Must have been jetlag. She didn't even look excited to see Tom, did she? So she must have been out of it. I tried to ring her later but her mum said she'd gone straight to bed as soon as she got back home.'

'Mmm. You would have thought she'd have looked a *bit* pleased, I mean seeing *Tom* again. And seeing Gregg. I know she'd met him already, but she hardly looked thrilled to be seeing a major star in your garden, did she? I hope everything's OK.'

I laughed. 'What are you on about? Of course everything's OK. She might have been a bit star-struck, that's all.'

'It's just that she was acting strange around Tom even before we all went away. Like she might not be so keen on him any more . . . Did you notice?'

'No! I didn't!' But I felt a twinge of anxiety, because secretly, maybe I had. 'You're imagining things, Rani.' I laughed it off.

'She's fine. Just jetlagged, like I said.'

Rani said she hoped I was right.

'Of course I am. Just wait and see, we'll *all* be back to normal in a day or two.' But when I said it I had my fingers crossed. I didn't want anything to change with the people I care about.

Which reminded me that I was getting nervous about seeing Jack later on. It had been such a long time. I hoped everything *was* going to be the same.

I cleared my throat. 'Hem hem. Talking of Gregg, Rani, did you notice how nice he was being?'

'Absolutely! Talk about charming.'

'No! I mean yes, but did you notice how he was being extra nice to anyone *in particular*?'

'No. He seemed to be being nice to everyone,' she said firmly.

This was not the response I expected, but then again, I wasn't sure what response I wanted so I wasn't upset when we were disturbed by screams of excitement from the hall. The star of the show had arrived.

We ran up on to the stage, grabbing Chloe on the way and got there in time to witness Gregg being mobbed by gangs of jumping, hysterical girls with Miss Lamb flapping around the outside trying to calm everyone.

Gregg was wearing long navy surfer shorts, trainers and a pale blue denim shirt that made his eyes look bluer than ever. He glanced up from the middle of the mayhem, spotted us and waved. 'Hi!'

A sea of girly faces turned to look up at us.

'Hi!' I called back as casually as I could. Oh, yes. That was my moment. That was what I had dreamed of. Carrie Henderson, friend to the famous.

Miss Lamb then did a lot of hand clapping and restored order. 'Now,' she boomed, 'we're very, very lucky to have Gregg Madison here with us. He is over in England to be in a film. He has very kindly agreed to lend us his expertise and help us with the auditions for our little performance.'

'Thank goodness no one knew this before today or else every girl in the country would be here,' Rani whispered. 'It would be like *X Factor* madness. In fact, why *is* he here?'

I blushed. I think I knew the answer to *that* one.

'It is *X Factor* madness already,' I managed to reply, watching Donna and Shanaid elbowing everyone else out of the way. Talullah was watching astonished from the sidelines (her mum had been sworn to secrecy) next to an amazed-looking Florence.

'Now, Gregg,' Miss Lamb's voice rose again, 'we probably need another person to help us with auditions.' She looked up at us on the stage and turned back to him. 'Would you like to choose someone?'

Gregg looked up again and this time I knew I wasn't imagining it. He was looking directly at *me*.

*Moi.*

Yours Truly.

'Carrie? Would you help me out?' he drawled.

Sitting in on auditions with Gregg Madison? Life just doesn't get any better.

'Boo,' Rani muttered. 'Now I'm lugging scenery around on my own.'

'It's only for one morning,' Chloe said crisply.

She *was* in a weird mood. I guessed she must have been disappointed Gregg didn't chose her. I mean, who wouldn't be?

Mum is yelling up the stairs about supper.

## 9.00 p.m.

Shepherd's pie. My favourite. Mum asked how the course had been and I told her I had helped Gregg choose who got the main roles. Ned said how could that be when I sing like a crow?

I ignored him.

He cannot help being jealous.

He must sense that my charisma is at an all-time high.

We had auditions all morning. We sat in a panel like on TV but we weren't allowed to make any comments after each person had done their little acting and singing bit. Mrs Lamb said we would make notes and talk about it afterwards, as they were all a bit young for harsh criticism, which I suppose was true. I do not want to be the person to tell eight-year-old Nicki Zuckerman that when she sings she reminds me of someone I love very much. My dad.

At the end of the morning, Chloe and Rani came up to where I was talking with Miss Lamb. Gregg was surrounded by girls, signing autographs. 'We're off outside now. Tom's waiting,' Rani said. So I said goodbye to Miss Lamb, waved at Gregg and we walked out into the bright summer sunshine.

I didn't know what to think. Gregg had just been so *nice* to me all morning. Really respecting my opinion and listening to what I had to say. And now I was going into town to meet Jack. I had no idea how I was going to feel when I saw him. It seemed so long ago since I last felt his arms around me, kissed him . . . What if it wasn't the same?

At the end of the path stood two figures.

'Ahh,' Rani sighed. 'So sweet. It's Tom, come to pick you up, Chloe.'

Chloe must still have been jetlagged because she just gave a small smile and said, 'Who's that with him?'

I took a couple of steps forward and my heart leapt as I recognised a familiar figure. And at that exact moment all thoughts of Gregg Madison flew out of my head. And I knew in an instant that there was only one boy in the world for me. My legs began flying down the path and I could hardly breathe as I flung myself into Jack's tall, lean gorgeousness. 'You didn't say you would meet me here!' I laughed, pushing his long, dark hair out of his lovely familiar intense brown eyes. I couldn't believe that for one tiny minute I could have imagined wanting to be with anyone else. How foolish was I? I kissed him. Nope, no one else's head appeared. Just Jack. Thank goodness he was back.

'I wanted to surprise you.' He grinned, pushing me away from him but holding on to my hands. 'Now let's have a look at you . . .'

'Carrie! Carrie!'

We all looked up. Gregg was running out of the hall calling out my name. He saw me and caught us up, slightly breathless.

'Carrie, I —'

'Gregg, this is Jack, Carrie's boyfriend,' Chloe interrupted, rather unnecessarily I thought. I *can* speak for myself.

Gregg stared at her briefly and paused.

'Hi,' he said, smiling at Jack. Which should have been Jack's opportunity to say how great it was to meet him and how much he liked his work.

'Hi,' Jack replied, not smiling quite so much as I expected. 'You wanted to say something to Carrie?'

There was rather an awkward pause. 'Yeah . . . Well, it was nothing important.' Gregg looked uncomfortable. 'Hey! Look, my ride is here. Got to go.' Mona was sitting in a car across the road. 'See you guys tomorrow. And thanks, Carrie, it was fun today, wasn't it?'

I nodded and waved as he crossed the road.

'What was fun?' Jack let go of my hands.

'We auditioned everyone for parts in *Cinderella*. You know, for Miss Lamb's play at Moulton Fair.'

'What's *he* doing auditioning people?'

'He volunteered,' Tom said. 'Very kind of him, considering. I mean, we still can't work out why he wanted to do it . . .'

'Really?' Jack's response had a *tone*.

'Are we going to the Coffee Bean or not?' Chloe snapped.

I caught Rani's eye in an 'Oo-er – what's up with her?' way and we set off. As arranged, I saw Talullah get into her mum's car. She leaned out of the window and yelled across the road.

'Is that your boyfriend, Carrie?'

I nodded, laughing.

'He's scrumptious!' she yelled back at me as the car drove off.

I spotted Donna and Shanaid glaring after her. Talullah had got the part of Cinderella.

*★* **CHLOE'S TIP:** •••••••••••••••••••

*Long journeys can leave you looking and feeling bedraggled.*
*Dress comfortably, leave your hair loose and don't bother*
*with make-up — if you sleep for a while in make-up it*
*can wreak havoc with your skin. Keep a refreshing face*
*spray, pressed powder, lip-gloss and a hairbush in your bag*
*though. Use them at your destination to feel fresh and*
*ready to face the world.*

# Chapter 8

Tuesday 8.30 a.m.

Rani rang last night.

'I think I see what you were getting at,' she said.

'About what?' I replied.

'About Gregg liking someone in *particular*.'

'I KNOW! You see it now?'

'What do you think he was going to ask you when he came running out of the hall? To go on a date?'

'I don't know! But *honestly*.'

'So what are you going to do? I thought you were nuts about him . . .' she said slyly.

'No! Not seriously. It *was* just a crush. I was *dazzled* by his fame, that's all. I *do* think he's a really nice person and of course he's gorgeous, but as soon as I saw Jack standing there I realised *exactly* how much I cared about him . . .'

'Phew! That's a relief.'

'I hope Jack realised it too.'

'I hope so. You could see that Jack wasn't too keen on the most desirable boy in the world running up and shouting your name for all the world to hear . . .'

'It was a bit awkward, wasn't it?'

'So you can't really blame Jack for being, well . . . *surprised*,'

Rani went on. 'But he's got nothing to worry about now, and he did *definitely* thaw out in the Coffee Bean later, didn't he?'

I felt a rosy glow of happiness. 'Yes, he did.'

'So the "Gregg's the most amazing boy I've ever met" phase is officially over now?'

'Yep.'

'You mean that?'

'Well, he'd have to take me in his arms and snog me passionately for me to really know for sure.'

Rani gave a horrified gasp. 'You *are* joking!'

'Of course I am.'

'I hope so! You mustn't let yourself get into a situation when he might get the chance to woo you with his film-star kissing. He must not lure you from your true love. If Gregg keeps making it so obvious he wants some personal time, hem hem, with you, it's not going to be very good for your relationship with Jack, you know.'

'I know! And I get the feeling that Gregg hasn't given up trying to get me on my own. Though he hasn't been successful in that yet, there are too many people around. I don't want to upset Jack about this. He's only just come back and we haven't seen each other for ages. I don't want him to get annoyed about *anything*.'

'You're quite Miss Irresistible these days, aren't you?' Rani sighed. 'It's so totally unfair. You have two gorgeous boys mad about you and I haven't got one. Where's the justice in that?'

'I cannot help being a siren for all menfolk. It is a power that has only recently come upon me and I must learn to deal with it responsibly.'

Rani blew a raspberry down the phone.

'There's only one thing for it, Carrie, you've got to put Gregg off somehow. Let him get the message.'

'How? I am what I am.'

'Well, be a bit less of it, then. Leave your hair unbrushed and don't wash it, let the grease show through a bit. Absolutely no make-up and wear your faded pink joggers and that shapeless red T-shirt.'

'Hey! I love that T-shirt.'

'It's hideous.'

'What!'

'Someone had to tell you. Now I've solved your problem, and I'm bored talking about boys liking you. Tell me about the auditions instead.'

So I did.

Yikes! Look at the time. Got to go and pick up Talullah.

 MADDY'S TIP: • • • • • • • • • • • • • • • • • • • •

Give your skin, hair and nails a break once in a while. Ditch the make-up, polish and styling sprays from time to time and let your skin and nails breathe, and your hair's natural oils work their conditioning magic. If you really want to bring out your natural glow, drink more water, and eat more fruit and vegetables too.

# Chapter 9

Tuesday 6.00 p.m.

Talullah went, 'Urgh! I see we're not at home to Miss Pretty today, Carrie,' when she opened the door this morning. I had taken Rani's advice seriously. It could not be denied, I was not looking my best. Talullah looked me up and down.

'Just a teeny hint, Carrie, girl to girl. Simply because you've been with someone for a while, it's no excuse to *let yourself go*. Or are you *trying* to get Jack to dump you? Because I think it might work.'

And I felt a flash of alarm, because I remembered that Jack had said he would pick me up outside the hall after the course today and we'd go into town and catch a film. There was no way I wanted him to see me in total slob mode.

I phoned him there on Talullah's doorstep to say I'd meet him at the cinema instead. Then I could dash back to my house and grab some decent clothes and make-up.

'But why?' he asked when I called. 'I don't mind coming to pick you up. I mean, I *want* to come and pick you up.'

'No, honestly, don't bother. I'd rather meet you in town.'

'Why?' he asked again, sounding suspicious.

'No reason, just it's a drag for you . . .'

'Is Gregg coming in today?'

'Yes, but that's nothing to do —'

'Is Tom coming to pick up Chloe?'

'Er . . . not sure.'

He gave an exasperated sigh. 'Look, Carrie, you know my dad wants to take me on this male-bonding camping trip for a few days. I've got a load of stuff to organise. Let's leave it today, all right?'

'But Jack! You've only just got back! I really wanted to see —'

'I'll see you tomorrow, OK? That's if you can fit me in. Bye.' He cut me off.

'Oooh.' Talullah frowned, looking troubled. 'Everything OK?'

'It will be.' I sighed. It can be very hard doing the right thing sometimes. I mean I was walking along the high street looking hideous in full view of the world, and all for who? Jack. That's who. I cheered myself up with the thought that after today everything would be sorted and back to normal again. I would make it up with Jack. I pulled myself together and turned to Talullah. 'Congratulations on being Cinderella by the way. And did I spot you chatting away with Florence . . .?'

'I love Florence!' She beamed. 'She's cool.' And then her normally merry eyes narrowed. 'Not like some of those girls . . .'

I felt a showdown coming on.

### 6.15 p.m.

Mum has just been in with *Celebrity* magazine. She said she would never normally read such a thing (a lie – you should see her at the dentist's) but there was a great photo of Gregg in it and an article about his forthcoming role in *Robin Hood*. No doubt about it, he is gorgeous but after what happened later this morning I'm not sure that I'll read it.

*6.25 p.m.*

OK. I did read it, though I don't feel quite the same way about Gregg Madison after what happened this morning.

Rani got the giggles when she saw me and couldn't stop the whole way to the hall. Not even when Donna was being dropped off and Jet leaned out of the car and yelled, 'Going for the natural look today, then, Carrie?'

I ran inside. I was surprised to see Mona Laverne, Gregg's publicity woman, standing talking to a slightly anxious-looking Miss Lamb. I wondered what Mona was doing there. I couldn't see her mucking in and making the little white mice masks. I had designed them for the Year Threes, which was the first task of the morning. In Miss Lamb's arts and drama course, for 'arts' read: 'Making Props for the Show'.

Gregg gave his usual cheerful wave and honestly didn't really seem to notice I was looking revolting. I wondered if his attraction was so strong he was beyond mere appearances. My task looked like it might be harder than I thought.

Rani nudged me. 'Look over there . . .' I turned to see Donna and Shanaid staring at Talullah who had bounded cheerfully up to greet Florence. They turned their backs and began whispering to their little gang. 'There's going to be trouble.' Rani shook her head. 'Let's make sure we're sitting with the Year Sixes this morning. We may need to referee.'

'Not if Talullah has anything to do with it.' I grinned. 'I don't think Donna has a clue who she's dealing with.'

'Are you coming?' Gregg was behind me. 'I can't stay long this morning and was kind of hoping we'd be on the same table.'

Rani's eyes went as wide and huge as they could possibly go in *a meaningful way*. Luckily Gregg didn't notice. I took a deep breath. I never actually imagined I would find myself in a situation where I was trying to put off Gregg Madison, but there I was. Call me Miss Charisma.

Even looking at his beautiful features and his perfect white teeth smiling at me, I knew what I had to do.

'No, I can't today, I'm on mice masks with Rani. I'm sure Chloe would love to help you out with the little ones on her outfit table, though.' I grabbed Chloe as she wandered past carrying a roll of pink felt for mice noses.

I have to say he seemed rather more pleased with this idea than I expected. Maybe my slob outfit had got to him after all. Chloe said they had enough help on her table. She *was* acting strangely these days: normally Chloe is the friendliest girl in the world and hates people being left out.

We had asked and asked if she was all right and she kept saying she was fine, but Rani and I decided it couldn't be still be jetlag. Rani disturbed me by saying again that it might be something to do with Tom but I told her that that was ridiculous. Chloe and Tom have been together forever, they're like best friends. They're *my* best friends. I really believed that once I had managed to shake off the attentions of Gregg we'd all be back to normal. Chloe and Tom. Jack and me.

In the end, Mr Hopper grabbed Gregg to help move some of the larger pieces of scenery into the hall while Rani and I sat with the Year Six gang. I noticed Donna eyeing Florence and Talullah in a hostile fashion as they sat down. Florence was wary as she began cutting the mask shape out of the card template. Talullah was totally relaxed. The other girls and Jeremy looked nervously at their leader, waiting for her to say something. They didn't have to wait long.

Donna turned and said loudly to Shanaid, 'Don't you think that *acting* isn't just about well . . . acting. It's what you *look* like too.' She gave her long blond hair a shake. 'Some people might be able to act and sing and stuff, but, kind of look all wrong for a part . . .'

Shanaid took it up. 'You mean like some people look like Cinderella . . .'

'Yes, and some people,' Donna flashed a glance down the table at Florence and Talullah, 'look like the ugly sisters . . .'

She began to giggle and rest of the table followed nervously. Emma and Jeremy, the ones who had *really* got the parts of the ugly sisters, were definitely giggling less enthusiastically but didn't dare to to spoil Donna's insult and annoy their leader. Florence went scarlet. I was going to intervene, but Talullah got there before me.

'Mmm . . .' she said calmly. 'So what are you saying here, Donna? That I don't fit into your idea of what Cinderella should look like? Is that what you're saying?'

Donna looked uneasy. She's not used to her victims answering back. The others were looking at her now, waiting. She shrugged her shoulders with a languid fake lack of concern before leaning forward and saying, '*Actually*, Talullah, if you don't mind, I was having a *private* conversation. Don't you know that it's very *rude* to eavesdrop on other people's conversations?' She looked triumphantly around the table for approval from the others.

Talullah beamed. 'Oh, *I'm* sorry, Donna. It's just that your voice is so *very* loud and so *very* piercing it really wasn't possible not to hear what you said. Can I give you a helpful tip for the future: with a voice like yours, if you want a private conversation, you really should go somewhere where people can't hear you.' She carefully dabbed some glue on her mask. 'Like Alaska or Australia or somewhere . . .'

Jeremy spluttered into a giggle. Donna's mouth opened and closed, but before her brain could compute a suitable answer a blinding flash dazzled us all.

A man was taking photographs. Gregg was standing with a group of children around him and another man was interviewing him. The photographer was now at our table and snapping at random. There was only one thing for me to do. I leapt up and ran for cover. After a frantic dash, I hid in the broom cupboard. There was no way anyone was going to take a photo of me today. Not looking as revolting as I did.

About ten minutes later I heard Gregg softly calling my name. I crouched down in the mops and wondered when that boy would leave me alone! Even looking my worst he cannot resist me. And the next thing I knew the door was opening. I scrambled to my feet. Now there's not a lot of space in that cupboard. Snug was the word. I knew this was it. He was going to make his move. The ultimate test of my love for Jack was about to happen. I braced myself for a fight.

'Carrie,' he said, standing very close, and closing the door behind him. 'Carrie, look, I expect you've kind of noticed, but I've been trying to talk to you alone.'

'Mmm,' I replied, backing into a collapsing pile of brooms.

'I realise you must know how I feel. I need to ask what you think about —'

'No, you don't!' I squeaked. 'I think you seem be a really nice person, but you have to understand that when people care about someone else . . . Well they just do and —'

'But do they?' Gregg was staring at me intently. 'Or are they just hanging on to a relationship that's run its course and staying due to guilt because they have such a gentle, kind personality, instead of taking a leap into something new . . .' He took another step forward.

'Er . . . *what*?!' I gulped. 'I don't think —'

'It's like we're both here in England now, and we both know how we feel. I *know* there's something special between us . . .'

'Well, hang on a bit there,' I protested.

'I mean I just *have* to know what you . . .' and he leaned right in.

*Oh my God! This is it!* I thought, and instead of wanting to fall into his arms and snog his face off, all I could think of was Jack's face and eyes and smile and how I honestly and truly didn't want to kiss anyone else.

'No!' I shrieked, pushing him backwards into the cleaning rags. 'No! I'm sorry but I'm with Jack. He's the only one for me. And nobody is going to take me away from him. I'm sorry, Gregg, but there is *nothing* special between us! You must forget about me . . .'

Gregg stepped back with a look of astonishment on his face.

'Forget about *you*? I know you're with Jack!' he cried. 'I want to talk to you about Chloe.'

'Chloe?' Now I was totally confused.

'Yes, Chloe. I'm crazy about her, you must have noticed . . .'

'Er . . . no, not really,' I replied, trying to gather my senses.

He looked astonished.

'She hasn't *told* you about us yet? I thought you were, like, best friends.'

Well so did I. I managed to speak again. 'What do you mean "Told you about us yet?". She hasn't said a word. What do you mean "*us*"? She's with Tom. Like I'm with Jack.'

Gregg looked troubled. 'When we met in LA, it was like there was this immediate connection between us . . .'

What Gregg was saying was beginning to register properly now and I was starting to get a grip on the situation.

'Gregg, listen, I think *every* boy Chloe meets wants to have an immediate connection with her. I expect a lot of girls *you* meet feel the same way about you. Practically *every* girl you meet,' I went on. 'Doesn't mean to say you feel the same way about *them*.'

'I do meet a lot of girls, Carrie, but not like Chloe. She's not like anyone I've ever met before. She's kind and gentle and hasn't a clue how amazing she is. She's so . . . so . . . special.'

'But she's Tom's girlfriend! She'd never leave him. Not for you, not for anyone!'

'But I'm sure we felt the same way about each other, Carrie. She did say she thought she was coming to the end of her relationship with Tom but now I'm here and they're still together and I don't get it. She won't even *talk* to me.'

'Because she doesn't feel the same way. And maybe she *did* seem to be different in America. You have to understand it was just a *crush*!' I replied. 'A mad moment of craziness. Not the real thing. And

I promise you, I *really* know what I'm talking about. Look, I don't know what you think happened in LA but I can assure you, you got it all wrong. Now she's back in England and has seen Tom again she's realised that it is him she wants to be with, always has. They're together forever . . .'

His eyes clouded over. 'You really think?'

'I absolutely one hundred per cent really think. No, not think. I *know*.'

'And you're, like, one of her best friends, right?'

'There is nothing I don't know about what she feels.'

'Except you don't actually know how she feels about this, do you?' He frowned. 'She hasn't said a word to you about any of this, has she?'

'Er . . . no. But I'm sure I know what she *will* say when I ask her.'

Gregg sighed. 'Guess I'll have to see how she responds to my letter, then.'

'What letter?'

'The one I sneaked into her bag this morning. I've just got to find out what's going on in her head. I don't have her mobile number, she wouldn't take mine. Hey, you couldn't give me her number, could you?'

We heard a sharp voice calling Gregg's name and I pushed past him out of the broom cupboard and into the hall. Gregg followed. Mona was standing outside, frowning. 'There you are! The photographer wants a final picture before we have to go, Gregg. Then we *really* have to go.' She looked around coldly at the tables full of excited and chattering children. 'You have a first script read-through in London to get to, so you're not going to be around for a few days.' She took him firmly by the arm and led him outside to where I could see the photographer waiting, leaving me with my mind in a whirl.

Tom and Chloe, Chloe and Gregg. It was so confusing and so disturbing, it's no wonder I did what I did.

Anyone in my position would have done the same.

### 7.15 p.m.

I needed to fortify myself with half a packet of digestives before I could write the next bit. I'm still not sure what I did was me at my wisest. It just seemed to me to be the only thing to do at the time.

After Gregg had driven off with Mona, I went back to join Rani and the others. I was still in a daze.

Florence, who was fairy godmother, and Talullah had been taken out for rehearsals.

Donna and her crew were looking rather subdued.

'First round to Talullah methinks,' Rani whispered to me, then noticed my expression. 'Hey! Where did you disappear to, anyway? And why do you keep staring at Chloe in that weird way?'

I could see Chloe pinning clothes on to some of the younger children on the other side of the room.

I thought I knew her inside out! I thought she was one of my best friends in the world. How could she have kept the Gregg thing a secret from Rani and me?

'I'll tell you in private later,' I murmured.

I tried to work it all out as I made wire whiskers and cut black-felt ears. And I did. I realised exactly what had happened. Chloe had been like me. She had thought she really liked Gregg, been dazzled by his fame and success, then come back to England, seen Tom again and realised her terrible mistake. She was probably rather embarrassed about the whole thing. Which is why she hadn't mentioned it. I had quite cheered myself up by the time we had cleared up and were walking out into the sunshine.

Tom was waiting for Chloe at the gate.

Tom surprised me as we approached by frowning at me disapprovingly. I didn't think it couldn't be my appearance – Tom doesn't notice things like revolting joggers and horrible hair. He only notices Chloe. I'd have to be wearing a rabbit suit or a paper bag over my head for him to spot there was anything different about me today and even then . . .

'Why didn't you want Jack to come and pick you up?' he cried. 'What's going on?' He looked meaningfully at the door of the hall where Gregg had appeared the day before.

'Nothing!' I smiled. 'Just thought I'd save him the extra journey. I'll see him tomorrow and everything will be fine.'

Everything *was* fine now. No more secrets and subterfuge. Everything was going to be just great! Gregg was on his way to London. We could all get back to normal.

'I've been meaning to ask you all morning,' Chloe said, who *does* notice everything about everyone's appearance, 'what's with this new, er . . . I hesitate to use the word "look"?' Her eyes flicked over me again. 'Especially that T-shirt?'

'Hey!' I exclaimed. 'I overslept, OK?'

'Well, don't do it too often,' she said laughing. 'Anyway, I've got a new lipstick that might help improve things a bit. God knows you need all the help you can get. Let me find it . . .'

And she began rummaging in her bag and as she did so a large white sheet of paper fell out. I had only time to read *Dear Babe*, before a breeze picked it up and scudded it along the path.

Tom took off after it before I could even think.

'Whoops! I've got it!' he yelled, eventually catching it by banging a foot down and trapping the paper. He scooped it and began to walk slowly back to us, glancing down at the page. Immediately he slowed down even more. He was now reading it intently, his face turning to stone.

As he came up to us, staring at Chloe, I realised there was only one thing for me to do. I grabbed the piece of paper out of his fingers, saying, 'Sorry, Tom, that's mine! I put it in Chloe's bag for safe keeping. Got to go now. Bye!'

And I grabbed Rani's arm and dragged her, protesting, along the road with me while Tom and Chloe stared after us.

Rani shook my arm off by the second lamp post. 'What are you *doing*?! You total nutter!' she shrieked.

'Shhh . . . Listen to me, Rani. No. Don't listen, look. Aargh! Don't look *back*! See!' And I thrust the letter into her hand. 'It's from Gregg!'

Rani read it out loud.

'*Dear Babe,*

'*I didn't want to contact you this way but I am going crazy that you won't speak to me. After meeting you in Los Angeles I haven't been able to think of anything else but you. Everything I said to you on the beach that last night was true and I hope that everything you said to me was true as well.*

'*I know that you don't want to hurt anybody's feelings but you did*

*say that you felt your relationship was coming to an end with your
boyfriend and that you were going to finish it when you got back. I know
you are wary of me because you think I'm famous and all that crazy
stuff, but you don't need to be. Please trust me – I'm just a regular guy
like any other, and if I know one thing, it's that I want to be with you.
I've never been more serious. Please, please believe me.*

'I know something important happened between us in Los Angeles.
I hope you still know it too. I won't give up on this. I can't.

'Gregg.

'Xxxx.'

By the time she had finished Rani was *vibrating* with emotion.
She raised her arm and began to flail at me with the letter.

'You, you . . . *lied* to me.'

Swish went the paper on my arm. Luckily for me, a piece of
paper is not a very effective weapon.

Holding it with two hands, she flipped it repeatedly on my
nose. 'You-said-you-never-met–him-in-Los-Angeles!'

'I didn't!'

Flap, flap, flap, now up on my forehead.

'My best friend! Oh my God, all that "Fate-is-always-so-against-
me-Gregg-arrived-in-LA-the-day-after-we-left." IT WAS ALL A BIG
LIE! You had planned to finish with Jack all along . . . you . . . you
. . . hypocrite!'

I grabbed the letter before she could inflict any real damage.
Like a paper cut.

'No! NO! You don't understand. The letter wasn't to *me*, Rani.
It was to *Chloe*.'

'Chloe?' The letter now hung in mid air.

I nodded. 'I spoke to Gregg in the broom cupboard. Well, it's a long story, but basically what he said was he's mad about *Chloe* and he thinks she feels the same. He put the letter in her bag. I didn't want Tom to know it was to her. *Something* happened to Chloe in Los Angeles . . . Gregg Madison bewitched her with his fame and fortune . . .'

Rani began to quiver again. 'She LIED to us! Our best friend! Oh my God . . .'

'We-ell. To be fair, technically she hasn't actually *lied*.'

'No wonder she's been in such a silent mood. She didn't want us to know.'

'I know. I think she realised she nearly made a big mistake and was ashamed to tell us.'

Rani gave me an odd look. 'Right. Well, whatever it is. I've had enough of it. NO MORE SECRETS! You and I are going to have a *serious* conversation with that girl.'

 CARRIE'S TIP: •••••••••••••••••

Take care of your appearance – make sure that your day to day clothes are in good condition, and remember that shapeless T–shirts just hang from your frame and are no one's friend.

# Chapter 10

**Wednesday 7.30 a.m.**

Rani and I went round to Chloe's yesterday evening.

Hang on. I'm just going to shut my bedroom door.

The bellowing bull is back again.

I am a stranger to a decent lie-in. And after what happened, I need my sleep.

We turned up at Chloe's house together. On the way there I filled Rani in on the broom cupboard conversation.

'Are you *sure* she's gone off Gregg?' Rani asked. 'She's not *acting* like she's got it all sorted. If she had, would she be so . . . well . . . unhappy-looking all the time?'

'It must be very awkward for her, Gregg turning up and being a pest. Attacking her *conscience*.'

'A pest! I never thought I'd hear you describe Gregg Madison as *that*!'

'Well, he is being one, isn't he? Not just leaving her alone . . . sending her stupid letters . . .'

'I thought it was quite a romantic letter . . .'

But Chloe had answered the buzzer by then so we shut up as we climbed the stairs to the top flat.

Chloe's brother Jim opened the door and flung himself cheerfully upon us asking a million questions about America and Disneyland and Universal Studios. Tom was nowhere to be seen, which was a relief. When we had finished with the hugging we looked up to see Chloe standing nervously behind Jim.

'Carrie,' she said, biting her lip. 'Carrie. I can't thank you enough for today. What you did, you know, about the letter. I found and read it this morning. It was kind of you to try and protect me . . . and don't worry, I swore Tom to secrecy.'

'You did what?'

'I made Tom swear not to tell Jack . . . you know, about the letter.'

'Well, thank goodness for that at least. Look, Chloe, I know things might have got somewhat complicated on holiday and *obviously* you don't want Tom to know. It would upset him for no reason. Couldn't you simply say to Tom that Gregg has been hassling you a bit but Tom's got nothing to worry about . . .'

She didn't answer. She looked at my bag. 'Have you got it?'

I gave her a steady look. 'Yes, I do.'

We stared at each other. 'Can I have it?' She held out her hand.

Rani pushed her way past us into the little sitting room. 'Not until you've given us some sort of explanation, Chloe. Carrie did a big thing for you today. I mean, what on earth has been going on?' She jumped up on to the sofa and tucked her legs under her. 'Come on then. Spill.'

I went and sat primly next to Rani with my bag on my knees. I tucked the letter back inside. Then we both stared at Chloe.

'All right, then,' she sighed, collapsing into the armchair opposite, 'but it's not what you think.'

'We don't know what to think yet,' Rani replied. 'So go on.'

'About Gregg. I know you must imagine, because of the letter, that something happened between us in Los Angeles.'

'And it didn't?!' I jumped up gleefully, forgetting to look disapproving. All was not lost.

'No. Well. Not like that.'

'Like what? Lip to lip contact you mean? Rani asked.

Chloe blushed.

Rani leaned forward. 'Did-you-snog-him?'

'No.'

'Kiss him without tongues?'

'Rani!'

Rani was undeterred. 'Details are important, Chloe. We have to know these things. Especially me – who will obviously never, ever get kissed, with or without tongues, and am doomed to die an old maid with only my cats around me. *Did* he try to snog you?'

'I told him I was still with Tom.'

'There you go!' I beamed triumphantly at Rani. 'I told you she wouldn't fall for him.'

'But I did,' Chloe said quietly.

I turned to her in astonishment. Poor thing, she wasn't thinking straight.

'No, you didn't. You *thought* you liked him and then you came home and realised you still wanted to be with Tom.'

'No, I didn't. I came back and ever since I got here it's been a total nightmare because I'm absolutely crazy about Gregg. You have to understand that I was already thinking about ending it with Tom before I went away . . .'

Rani gave me a triumphant 'I told you so' look, which I ignored.

'I can't bear the thought of hurting Tom, but from the first second I met Gregg I knew he was someone really special . . .'

'Yes, well, he *is* someone really special,' I interrupted. 'He's a famous TV star! But Chloe, *millions* of girls think he's special. But it's not *real*. He's not like, like a real person . . .'

'Actually he is . . .' Rani frowned. 'Everyone's a *real* person underneath, whatever they do. Except for Paris Hilton of course.'

I gave her a 'Whose side are you on?' look and swept on. 'Look, Chloe, I've got a confession. Gregg made *me* feel a bit, er . . . giddy for a while. But as soon as I saw Jack I knew what I had been feeling was nothing more than a crush. Pure and simple. A silly crush. Because he was good-looking and famous. And that was all it was. I didn't really *know* him. And that's all it is with you.'

'No, Carrie! It's not a crush. We got to spend a lot of time together in America. I could talk to him for ever. He's one of the most genuine people I've ever met in my *life*!'

I took a deep breath. 'The thing is, Chloe, the thing is . . . it's not surprising you imagine you've fallen for him. We come from a small village – God knows we don't have very glamorous lives – it's understandable that you would be dazzled by someone like Gregg and his Hollywood lifestyle. *Loads* of girls fantasise about being his girlfriend and living that life.'

'Are you saying I only like him because he's rich and famous?' Chloe's eyes flashed dangerously.

'Don't knock it! It would be good enough for me!' Rani cried.

'I'm saying you're not serious about him,' I wailed. 'Like I told him yesterday. You're with Tom. And you'd never leave him.'

Chloe went still. 'You told him *WHAT*?'

'Hey, Chloe,' Rani interrupted, 'to be fair to Carrie, she didn't have a clue about your, your . . . er . . . feelings about Gregg when she said what she did.'

Chloe ignored her. 'Do you know what I think, Carrie?' she said hotly.

'What?' I asked.

'I think you should try and think about this from someone else's perspective.'

'I am,' I said hotly. 'It's poor Tom's perspective *I'm* thinking about. *He's* crazy about you.'

Chloe suddenly looked like she was going to cry. 'Don't you think I know that, Carrie? But I can't help it if I don't feel the same way about him any more. It *was* a great relationship, but it's over now. I know that for sure. I did what I promised myself I'd do. I came back to England and I tried. I really tried. Do you know how hard it has been for me keeping away from Gregg? Avoiding him? It's been agony. But I did it, I did it out of respect for Tom, who I know is a lovely, lovely person, but it hasn't worked. This last afternoon together I knew it was pointless trying any more. I *know* I want to be with Gregg. I'm sorry if it spoils things for you, Carrie, I know you liked it being Jack and you, Tom and me, but I can't carry on going out with him just to please everyone else. I just can't!'

Rani stepped in. 'Look, Chloe, you're obviously upset, and of course you must do what you want to do . . .' She shot me a warning glare. 'We care about you. I mean, if Carrie didn't care about you she wouldn't have said that that letter was for her, to protect you.'

'From making a terrible mistake!' I shrieked. 'And I was

protecting Tom! Didn't you see his face? I had to do *something*.'

'Look, I said thanks, and I meant it.' Chloe sighed. 'I truly appreciate what you were trying to do, but I know what I'm going to do now. I'm going to tell Tom it's over. Tomorrow. OK? We're all meeting up in the Coffee Bean and I'm going to tell him I need to talk to him, we'll go to the park or something. This can't go on any longer. I've made my mind up and that's that.'

My hands went on to my hips: never a good sign. 'What! You're going to throw away your whole relationship with Tom, who you've been going out with for nearly two years, for some . . . some . . . poster-boy who you only met a week or so ago. Are you *totally* stupid?'

'Give me the letter please,' Chloe said darkly.

'You'll be making the biggest mistake of your whole life.'

'Give me the letter and then . . . and then I think you'd better go.'

'Chloe!' Rani exclaimed.

'I just want to be on my own now. Can you *please* give me that letter!'

I rummaged in my bag. 'OK! Here's your stupid letter,' I cried and threw it at her. 'But you're making the biggest mistake of your life!' And I scrambled up and stomped out of the door, followed by Rani.

I only stopped stomping when we got to the bus stop and Rani caught me up. She leaned against the side of the bus shelter.

'Well,' she said, wrinkling her nose, 'that could have gone better . . .'

RANI'S TIP: •••••••••••••••••••••

We all know Carrie is hardly a pro at keeping calm and giving her brain a rest, but there are simple things that can help:

1) Listen to her wise friend Rani.

2) Take a warm bath with relaxing lavender oil in it.

3) Drink camomile tea.

4) Do some exercise in the afternoon, so she feels naturally tired at the end of the day.

5) Turn her phone off from time to time. Or maybe that would stress her out more!

# Chapter 11

Thursday 12.00 p.m.

I'm watching the rehearsal at drama club, but all I can think about is that Chloe is going to finish with Tom this afternoon.

As if in sympathy with Tom, a light grey drizzle accompanied us on our way to the hall this morning.

'What's the matter *now*?' Talullah wailed at me from under her umbrella this morning. She is a very perceptive girl, but can lack sensitivity.

'Nothing,' I said grimly.

'Has Jack dumped you? I *told* you about letting yourself go. That T-shirt . . .'

'Will everyone please shut up about the T-shirt. Everything's fine with Jack and me.' I paused. 'Well, it will be this afternoon.'

Which is true, and why I've just spent ages and ages getting ready to see him. I am in my white denim skirt and blue shirt with my white ballet pumps. It is too wet for sandals. It is too wet for ballet pumps really, but I refuse to wear my trainers.

I feel I should really be top to toe in black. In mourning for Chloe's massive mistake. At least a lone black armband anyway. I don't know how I'm going to look Tom in the face when we walk into the Coffee Bean. Which will be in an hour.

Tom has only *one* solitary hour of happiness left to him.

Talullah continued to grill me when Rani joined us.

'Is it Chloe, then?' she went on. 'I noticed you dragging Rani off down the lane yesterday, leaving Chloe and Tom staring after you . . .'

She did an impression of wide staring eyes, mouths open in shock.

'*Thank* you,' Rani said. 'She *was* dragging me, wasn't she?'

'What's up with Chloe, then?' Talullah persisted.

'Nothing,' Rani and I chorused together.

'I see.' Talullah nodded. 'So it's boy trouble, then. Got to be something to do with boys, it always is. You say it's not Jack, though. So it must be Chloe and Tom.'

'Oh yes, thank you very much,' Rani said crisply. 'Couldn't possibly be *me*, could it? Couldn't be *me* with the romantic dilemma.'

'Is it?' Talullah frowned.

'No.' Rani sniffed. 'But thank you for asking.'

'You're *so* like my brother.' Talullah sighed.

'Great,' said Rani. 'And where *is* your brother, anyway? Where are you keeping him?'

'Science summer school in London – he's a bit of a brainbox.'

'So that's why you think he's like me?' Rani beamed. 'Because he's so brilliantly clever.'

'No, he's like you because he's always moaning about not having a girlfriend. But when girls do go for him, and for some mysterious reason they do, they're never quite right and he never goes out with anyone.'

'Well, that's certainly like you, Rani,' I said grinning.

'Can we get back to the point?' she said primly.

'Exactly! We were discussing Chloe and Tom,' Talullah said firmly. 'Are they splitting up?'

'Yes,' said Rani as I wailed 'No!' at the same time.

'Mmm.' Taluallah frowned. 'That clears things up, then . . .' But then we were at the gate to the hall.

Donna and Shanaid were being dropped off. They whispered something to each other as they got out of the car, and looked over. Talullah gave them both a cheerful wave which made Donna so furious that when April arrived, sharing an umbrella with Florence and chatting away, she got a daggers look from her leader and stopped talking mid-sentence, paralysed. Florence smiled at her. 'You go in,' she said. 'I'll go in with Talullah.' April gave her a grateful smile and ran inside.

'It's ridiculous!' Talullah cried, staring after her. 'She was scared to be seen even *talking* to Florence. Those girls daren't even breathe unless Donna approves.'

Florence sighed. 'I don't blame April. I know what it's like not to be "in" with Donna. It's not a nice place. Woodside is only a small village primary. If Donna decides you're not part of her group, life is pretty miserable. And I could never be one of the chosen ones. Not with my mum working in the village shop and me never having the right clothes, or hair.' She patted her head and grinned sheepishly at Talullah.

Talullah shook her own spiral corkscrew curls and put her arm through Florence's. 'Come on, we have rehearsals to go to, and you can say whatever you like about Miss Donna. The fact is *you're* the fairy godmother and get to wear a great dress, and she's Prince

Not Very Charming . . .' and they wandered into the hall.

I followed them in. I had to find Chloe.

She was already inside and didn't smile as I approached.

'Look, I was wondering if I could have a word,' I murmured.

'No,' she replied firmly, handing out white ribbons to her group of white mice.

'Please, Chloe. Just five minutes. Just to ask you to seriously *think* about what you're going to do today.'

'I've thought of nothing else day and night for weeks now, Carrie. There's nothing you can say to change my mind.'

'Five minutes,' I pleaded. 'Chloe! Please.'

'No.' She leaned across the table. 'Could you pass the scissors, Emma?' and she turned away.

I tried again, several times, but she wouldn't even look at me by the end of the morning. What the atmosphere is going to be like when I walk into the Coffee Bean I can't imagine. It's going to be like high noon in a cowboy film. At least Jack will be there. I am so looking forward to seeing him and putting everything right between us.

Things won't be the same without Tom and Chloe going out together as well though. I feel something safe and cosy is unravelling, and I don't like it.

Oops! Finale's beginning. Better get going then.


### 7.00 p.m.

I wish I had spent the afternoon doing something else. Like having root canal work at the dentist or having a Brazilian wax or something.

When I arrived at the Coffee Bean, Chloe wasn't there yet so I thought I'd wait outside as I didn't fancy seeing Tom on my own. I could see him watching me through the glass, though. I'd have to go in or else he'd know something weird was happening. I'd *never* usually wait for Chloe outside if one of our group was already there – that would have seemed very odd. I was also disappointed to see that Jack hadn't arrived yet. He's not usually late.

I took a deep breath and went in, paid for my hot chocolate and took it over to where Tom was sitting. He didn't give me his usual big smile. In fact, he looked at me with an unfriendly glare. I knew this was all about the letter. Honestly, you try and help someone out . . . At least *that* confusion would be cleared up soon. Not that it would make him feel any better.

As it was, he could barely look at me as I slipped into the seat opposite him. He stared at his glass of Coke instead.

I was just getting used to the idea that we'd sit in silence until Chloe or Jack arrived when he mumbled into his drink, 'Jack's not coming.'

'What?' I looked up. 'What do you mean he's not coming? Why?'

He slowly raised his head from his glass. 'I think you *know* why, Carrie.'

My head was beginning to spin a little. 'No, I don't, Tom. I really don't.' I looked up into Tom's accusing eyes and my heart jumped. 'Unless, unless . . .' My heart was racing now. 'Tom!' I hissed, glancing around me to check no one could overhear. 'Chloe said you *swore* you wouldn't say anything to Jack about the letter. You haven't, have you? Because you've got it so wrong; it wasn't what it sounded like at all . . . *Please* say you didn't . . .'

'Sounded like something to me, Carrie,' he answered coldlsy. 'I know I told Chloe I wouldn't say anything, but Jack phoned last night and was upset about how off you've been with him, saying he hoped you'd get it all sorted out today . . .'

'And we will!' I shrieked.

'I just couldn't keep him in the dark, Carrie. He's my mate and to be honest he kind of suspected it anyway, you know after Gregg came running out the other day and stuff . . . I *had* to tell him.'

My blood froze. 'You had to tell him *what*?'

Tom shrugged his broad shoulders uncomfortably. 'You know. About you and Gregg, in America.'

'What!'

'Honestly, Carrie, I . . . I *never* thought that you'd do something like this to Jack. He was pretty cut up. He said the one thing he never thought you were was a liar. You told him you didn't see Gregg in LA. Seems there can be only one reason why you didn't want him to know that you *did*. Honesty is really important to Jack. He says you're not the girl he thought you were.'

'But, it's not *true* – he's got it all wrong – I *never* met Gregg in America.'

'Don't keep on lying, Carrie. The letter said it all.' Tom now stared directly at me. 'He doesn't want to see you any more . . .'

'He never said that.'

'He did. I'm sorry Carrie but you can't blame the guy . . .'

But I wasn't listening by then. I was searching for my phone and scrambling to my feet. 'Where is he now?' I asked.

'Who?' Chloe was standing right behind me. I turned to her furiously.

'You may well ask!' I snapped. 'You may bloody well ask!'

And I ran out.

## 11.00 p.m.

I can't sleep.

I ran out of the Coffee Bean and got a bus straight to Pitsford. I ran all the way up the drive to Pitsford Hall and that is a long, long way, and banged on the door. Chloe's mum answered, and for a moment I was confused to see her there. It shows what a state I was in because she's worked as Jack's dad's personal assistant for ages now.

She told me Jack wasn't in. Nobody was in. Jack had persuaded his dad to leave on their male-bonding camping trip a day early. He'd be back in a few days.

A few days! And he wouldn't answer his phone. I had already tried eleven times.

I told Chloe's mum I had an absolutely *totally* urgent message for Jack and his phone wasn't working. Could she give me his dad's mobile? *Please!*

So she did and Jack answered. I could hear they were in his dad's car.

'Jack! Listen. Don't hang up. You must listen to me. What Tom told you – he got it all wrong. I never met Gregg in America! There is *nothing* going on between us . . .'

'Forget it, Carrie. I think the letter kind of said it all, didn't it? When *were* you going to finish with me exactly?'

'I wasn't!'

'Well, I've saved you the bother now, Carrie, haven't I?'

And he cut me off before I could say another word.

I totally and completely blame Chloe for this. She's making everything go wrong. I have never been so angry with anyone in my life.

 CHLOE'S TIP: • • • • • • • • • • • • • • • • • • • •
*Thinking about what you wear to impress someone is one thing, but other occasions matter too. If you dump someone, don't go looking glam and ready to pull someone new. Be sensitive and dress down a little.*

# Chapter 12

Chloe didn't turn up to Miss Lamb's today.

Rani and I went back to the scenery store and I apologised to her for phoning her so late last night.

'I just couldn't get to sleep.'

'Yeah, well, do you know something amazing, Carrie? I could. My phone didn't stop all evening! Let me see . . .' She began to count off her fingers. 'There was you, Chloe, Tom, you again, Tom again, Chloe twice more, Tom, Jackie from school asking me to go on the Alton Towers trip – what was all *that* about? – Tom again and then finally just after I had managed to drop off, you.'

'I'm so sorry. No Jack, then?'

'No Jack. But I hope that eventually, if one day – when I'm in the old people's home at the rate I'm going – I ever do get into a relationship that has problems, that you will all remember my kindness to you at this time.'

'We will, don't worry. And you will find someone you're crazy about really soon. I just know it. You do think Jack and I will get back together as soon as he realises what's happened, don't you?'

She looked up from painting pink roses climbing up a castle tower. 'I hope so.'

I sat back from sanding down the huge wooden moon. I was getting it ready to paint a pumpkin on one side and a coach on the other.

'You hope so!'

'I'm sure it will be fine, Carrie.'

'Tom was devastated, wasn't he?' It had been a horribly upsetting call when he'd phoned me last night to apologise about the misunderstanding, now that Chloe had told him the truth.

'He did say that he had tried to contact Jack to explain but his mobile's still off. It was really good of him to try, as heaven knows he has enough of his own woes to think about.'

'I know,' Rani sighed. 'Completely. I didn't know what to say to him except it won't always feel this bad. He was so upset. It'll take him a long time to get over it.'

'Unless he doesn't have to.'

'What do you mean?'

'We've got to get them back together. Simple. We have to save her from Her Hideous Mistake.'

Rani sat back and looked at me. 'Oh God, Carrie, I know what you're going to say next . . .'

'I have a plan.'

She waved her paintbrush in the air. 'Yup! That was it.'

'Gregg is away in London. Nothing has happened in the snogging department yet, so they're not *officially* together because everyone knows until you've kissed you're not actually going out together. *He* doesn't have her mobile number, she doesn't have his. He doesn't know she's finished with Tom. There's still time.'

'Time for what?'

'Aren't you listening? Time to make her realise Her Hideous Mistake.'

'And how do you intend to do that?'

'Yes, well, that's the bit I'm working on. I've made a list of "Things Tom Could Do To Make Chloe Realise Her Hideous Mistake".'

'Oh God. Are you serious?'

'Shall I tell you what they are or not?'

'Do I have a choice?'

'No.'

'Go ahead then.'

'One: make her jealous. Be seen with someone else. That's my best one, I think.'

'What's number two?' was Rani's response.

'Number two: do something seriously heroic.'

'Hmm. Go on . . .'

'Three: do something to make your rival look pathetic, mean or just plain bad.'

Rani said nothing but I sensed her disapproval.

'These are desperate times, Rani,' I said sternly. 'And I have one last one. Want to hear it?'

'Not really.' She was concentrating very hard on a rose.

'It's a lot harder to think of things than you might think, you know. I've put a lot of effort into this,' I snapped.

'Sorry. OK, go on . . .'

'Four: find a way of getting your rival to go away. Permanently. Which, before you say anything, Rani, would not be that impossible, because if Gregg went back to America it would solve all our problems.'

'And exactly how are you intending to do that?' Rani asked. 'Because I have to tell you that even with a lot of squishing he won't fit in a letterbox. And that's if he *wasn't* struggling – which would be unlikely in the circumstances.'

'Ha ha.'

She wiped her paintbrush with a rag. 'None of them will work, Carrie.'

'How can you be so negative? How do you know?'

'Chloe's not blinded by his good looks or interested in fame or money. You know she's not. If we had been paying attention, it was perfectly clear, even before she went to America, that she was coming to the end of her relationship with Tom. She did the decent thing and tried to give it one last go and it didn't work. She genuinely likes Gregg. I don't think it's a crush. I think it's the real thing. Trying to get her back with Tom would be a waste of time and may end up causing Tom more misery, because it won't work.' She jammed her brush back into the pot. 'No. I don't want any part of it. It's over, we have to accept it.'

I was staggered. 'But —'

'I don't want anything to do with it.'

'Well. I see,' I said. 'I see I'm the only one that cares enough to —'

'You have to accept *change*, Carrie. People *change*. Relationships end. New relationships begin, though obviously *not* in my case. You may not like it, *I* may not like it. We LOVE Tom and Chloe going out together, it feels comfortable and familiar, but we don't have the right to say they must stay like that forever.'

'So what are you saying? You won't help me? You won't help me try this one last time before Gregg gets back and all will be lost forever?'

'What do you mean lost forever? No, I won't.'

'So I'm on my own with this, am I?'

'Yes.'

'Right. I'll do it by myself.'

'OK.'

'Or get someone else to help me.'

'Fine by me.'

And then Miss Lamb appeared and said that she needed some help with the new Year Four bird costumes as Chloe wasn't in, and Rani and I were flat out measuring elastic round children's heads and fastening it on to yellow card beaks all morning.

Which was quite a relief really, as it had almost felt that Rani and I had been heading for a row.

And if she doesn't want to help me I can easily find someone else with the maturity and sensitivity to understand the situation who can.

 MADDY'S TIP: • • • • • • • • • • • • • • • • • • • • •
If you are able to tell when you and your friends are heading for a row, try and call a stop to the conversation. Chances are, you're all stressed about something and could use a few minutes' time out. It could save a big falling out.

# Chapter 13

Have just returned from sorting out Phase One of My Plan.

Luckily Talullah was in.

I got more than I bargained for because, when I rang her doorbell, her brainy brother answered. And he is not at all scrappy and grungy and sniggering like Ned's friends are.

Which is not surprising as although he isn't that tall, it turns out he is sixteen years old. How Mum got her facts so wrong I didn't know, especially as she had put so much ground work in on the spying and information-gathering. She must have made a guess from a distance. His hair is a shorter version of his sister's and he has his mother's melting brown eyes in smooth browny-golden skin. I can also report that he is well fit as he was only wearing a pair of jogging bottoms when he opened the door and I got a good look at his torso. He's called Drew. My heart may belong totally to Jack but I know a good-looking boy when I see one, even if he is about four inches shorter than me. Whatever his sister says about him, I do not believe he will be single long.

Which reminds me, I had a terrible nightmare about Jack last night. I dreamed that he refused to get back together with me, even though I explained that the 'Babe' letter wasn't to me and begged and begged. Woke up with my cheeks wet from crying and lay awake for several anxious hours staring wide-eyed at the ceiling thinking about how miserable I would be if we split up.

It did however make me even more determined to try and put my plan to get Chloe and Tom back together into action. I couldn't bear Tom feeling so unhappy. And Chloe disappearing to Hollywood with Gregg. Desperate times call for desperate measures.

'So *what* do you want me to do?' Talullah asked. I do hope she has the maturity and sensitivity for the task.

## 8.00 p.m.

To be fair, it wasn't Talullah's fault. She did do everything she was asked.

I had been forced to abandon the first item on my list – making Chloe jealous – as no one was going to believe that Tom had found new love with Talullah or anyone else.

I did think of Rani's cousin, Rukshana, who Rani tells me is up for most things and would do anything for a fiver, but

1. She lives in Sheffield, and

2. I'm not sure Rani would give me her number.

So I had to go straight to the second item on my list: make Tom a hero.

The way I planned it all was pure genius.

Luckily it was a sunny day as I wouldn't have liked to ask Talullah to wait up there in the rain.

The plan was simple but perfect.

I phoned Rani and Chloe and said, 'This is silly, let's all meet up at mine and we'll spend some time doing some beautification, just us. No discussion about boys allowed. I don't want any more fighting or bad feeling.' And they said they would both come and

Chloe said she was glad that I wasn't going to let this come between us.

Then I phoned Tom and asked him if he wanted to come round for a heart-to-heart and of course he said yes because everyone knows when your heart is broken you have to talk and talk about it. So I asked him to come fifteen minutes after Rani and Chloe.

Rani and Chloe arrived and I felt like James Bond. We went upstairs and when I looked out of my bedroom window I spotted a slight swaying at the top of the tree in the garden opposite. Talullah was now in position.

It was very hard to talk about eye-shadow when my ears were straining to hear what was happening outside. Luckily I didn't have to wait long. Rani and Chloe had barely flopped down on my bed when loud shrieks pierced the hot afternoon air.

'Help! Help!' (I have to say Talullah is a brilliant actress – so I was glad I had seen her brother go out and that her parents were right at the bottom of her back garden.)

'What's the matter? What's going on up there?' It was Tom's voice.

'Help me! Get me *down*!'

'Are you OK?' Tom's voice again. Rani shot me a glance but I shrugged my shoulders and gave her an 'I'm as astonished as you are – what a curious thing' look. We all ran to the window and looked out. Tom was standing at the bottom of the large oak in Talullah's front garden, peering up into the branches.

'What's he doing here?' Chloe frowned. 'I don't want to see him. He might get upset. It's so awkward at the moment.'

'I have no idea,' I replied. 'He's allowed to walk the street, I suppose. Must be on his way somewhere. Come on, let's go down. See what's happening.'

Rani and I ran down, with Chloe reluctantly tagging along behind. I noticed she didn't come over my front garden and cross the road with us, but waited in the doorway.

Never mind. Tom couldn't see her yet, but *she* could see and hear everything. Her hero.

'Hi, Rani,' he said, smiling. 'Didn't expect to see you —'

'ARE-YOU-ALL-RIGHT?' I yelled very loudly in an upwards direction.

'I'm too scared to come down by myself,' Talullah cried down. 'I've climbed up and can't move. I need someone to come up and help me. To talk to me, calm me down . . . I'm, er . . . I'm in a bit of a state.'

I looked expectantly at Tom.

'Hold on, Talullah!' Rani called up. 'You just wait there and I'll be up in a jiffy.' She headed towards the tree, tucking her skirt into her knickers.

'No!' Talullah yelled down again. 'No! I don't think you can make it, Rani, you're too small, not *strong* enough . . .'

'But you're even smaller than —'

'But that was the problem in the first place, Rani,' Talullah called down (that girl is a genius sometimes). 'I wasn't really big enough to take on a tree of this . . . this . . . *magnitude*. Save yourself, Rani. Don't make the same mistake I did.'

'Oh.' Rani stepped back, confused. I noticed Chloe was still keeping well away, but had stepped off the front step and on to the garden path.

'I think it really might need to be someone big and strong. I think it needs to be a man,' a voice wafted down wistfully.

We all looked at Tom, who didn't look that enthusiastic. Which was not good.

'Go on, Tom,' I whispered. 'You can do it.'

He turned to me, astonished. 'What? Climb up there? Are you kidding? That's a seriously tall tree.'

'It's not really, not at all,' I murmured. 'She's simply gone about it the wrong way. It's actually incredibly easy to get up. Ned climbs it all the time.' (Which was a lie and I felt a bit bad about that, but honestly – if Talullah could do it . . .)

'Does he?' Tom replied, brightening up a little.

'And it would look very brave . . .' I added in a meaningful voice, jerking my head in the direction of my front door.

When Tom saw Chloe, first of all he looked confused, then he went bright red, then he nodded at her and she nodded back. Chloe was right, it was awkward. But hopefully not for much longer, I thought.

'He-elp! Save meeee . . .' a pathetic wail came from above.

I guessed Talullah was getting slightly bored.

Tom looked at Chloe, looked up at the tree again, took a deep breath, and strode forward in a manly, purposeful manner.

Unfortunately that was the last of us seeing anything manly or purposeful, as we spent the next twenty-five minutes watching him red-faced, puffing and panting as he heaved himself slowly up the trunk, up through the lower branches and then almost out of view. He then came to a halt. Tom is a large boy, and I now officially know this for a fact: he is not an agile one. It was not exactly how I wanted Chloe to see him, but we hadn't got to the main rescue part yet, so I was still optimistic.

'Why have you stopped? Are you there yet?' Rani called up.

'Not quite,' he called back down. 'It's a lot further than you might think. I'm just catching my breath.'

'You might be able to talk me down from there,' a voice cried from a branch far above him. 'I think that might be exactly what I need. Please don't try and come up any further. I think your presence alone is giving me courage.'

'Really?' Tom asked, sounding relieved.

'Yes, you stay there and I'll come down to you. Then you can soothingly and bravely talk me down the last bit.'

Rani gave me a 'She's a bit weird' look, but I ignored it.

There was the sound of someone moving through the upper branches, and then silence. With our necks craned we could see Talullah's feet had joined Tom's sitting on a branch far, far above us.

We strained to hear a murmured conversation going on, but couldn't make out the words until Tom gave out a huge and, I have to say, unmanly shriek.

'GET OFF ME! I'M NOT LETTING GO!'

Then there was more murmuring. Then silence. For some time.

'Carrie?' Talullah's voice eventually gently wafted down.

'Yes?'

'I think Tom might be a little bit stuck.'

**CARRIE'S TIP:** ••••••••••••••••••••••

A fun session of beautification with friends can include anything from having facials, manicures, pedicures to practising
makeovers and outfits. To complete the fun, make the most of
the room you are in — have plenty of freshly washed towels ,
DVDs and magazines for ideas, cushions to get comfy and
music to get it all going!

# Chapter 14

Sunday 9.30 a.m.

Times I've tried Jack's mobile: 49.

It is not often that I lie in bed on a Sunday morning, with a slice of toast and cup of tea, and think about how very, *very* marvellous our fire brigade really is.

Because they were. They were great. Even if they did say we were lucky they were having a quiet day, because what if there had been a proper fire to go to, and they had been using the extending ladder thing on the top of the engine to heave Tom out of the tree, instead of putting out serious blazes?

Which was a good point. And has made me realise that the 'Make Tom a Hero' plan had perhaps not been as well thought out as it might have been.

Talullah scrambled down quite happily in a couple of minutes, of course, so her parents were bemused to come out into their front garden to find a strange boy up their tree and a fire engine parked outside. The driver didn't do the siren – he said it wasn't an 'emergency'. Well, excuse *me*, I think Tom would beg to differ. By the time Tom was safely in the basket thing on the top of the ladder with the nice fireman, quite a crowd had gathered and Chloe said she felt she'd better go and would Rani go with her and they left before he'd even been lowered to the ground.

You see, *this* is what it's going to be like with Chloe not going out with Tom. We'll never be able to hang out all together again. It will be the start of our friendship group breaking up. And I can't bear it.

'You did a very silly thing, Carrie,' Mrs Banks told me, offering me a cup of tea in her kitchen. Tom was recovering over in my house – I'd left him in front of a DVD. I'd made an excuse about checking if Talullah was OK but really I knew I had to confess to her parents that it was all my idea. Tom had to tell the fire brigade why he was up there, and I couldn't let Tallulah get into any trouble because of me. She didn't want me to own up, but when I told her that she could still keep the bag of outgrown clothes I'd promised her, she was OK about it.

'It could have been very dangerous.' Mrs Banks frowned. 'I'll have to tell your parents.'

I nodded. 'I know.' I was grateful Mum and Dad were out till late that night. 'It was an incredibly stupid idea.'

'Poor Tom.' Mrs Banks shook her head. 'Have you told him what it was all about? He should know.'

'I'm just going to,' I said, downing my tea.

But when I got back, the first thing Tom did was look up from the sofa and say, 'Well, she's never going to go back out with me now, is she? I made a right fool of myself. Why didn't I admit that I was afraid of heights? I can't believe I was such an idiot.'

'You weren't an idiot at all . . .' I whimpered.

'And when Talullah got her nerve back and scampered down in three minutes flat, well . . . I couldn't believe it.' He sighed. 'On the other hand, maybe my being up there *did* help her.'

'I'm *sure* it did.' I patted his arm. 'I'm sure it made all the difference.'

'Any luck getting hold of Jack?' he asked.

'No.'

'Me neither.' It was his turn to pat my arm. 'Don't worry, Carrie. As soon as he hears it was all a mistake, he'll be fine.' He looked so hurt for a moment, but gathered himself and glanced at his watch. 'Better go. Going to help my dad get the stage ready for Moulton Fair.' And he went, leaving me feeling totally terrible.

I *couldn't* tell him that it was me who'd caused the disastrous events of the afternoon.

I have made things worse not better. Instead of thinking of Tom as a hero, Chloe will be thinking exactly opposite. I have practically pushed her into Gregg's arms, not snatched her from them.

I *have* to make things up to Tom somehow.

## 2.30 p.m.

Have just returned to my room after a long session in the kitchen with Mum and Dad. Mrs Banks, true to her word, had a chat with them on the phone this morning. I won't dwell on the conversation. Needless to say it was painful, guilt-inducing and involves me having to stay in all day, no visitors allowed and no allowance money till I'm practically dead.

Times I've tried Jack's mobile: 67.

Rani rang and asked if I'd meet her and Chloe at the Coffee Bean. They are the *last* people I want to know what really happened so I said I wasn't feeling well and was staying in bed. She said she'd call later and see how I was. She is a true friend.

### 3.00 p.m.
JACK RANG!

He and his dad are back from their rugged male-bonding camping trip. Jack has spoken to Tom. Everything is OK between us. I felt so relieved I had to do a little dance around my room.

'Shall I come straight round?' he asked after we'd said all the things I'd hoped we'd say in that phone call.

I stopped my skippy-dancing abruptly.

'Er . . . no, not such a good idea today,' I replied.

'You're kidding me,' he wailed. 'What's up now?'

'I'm grounded.'

'Grounded! Why? Oh God, what have you done?'

'I haven't done anything, Jack.' I paused. 'Except try to help others.'

'Help others? That sounds bad. Who?'

'Tom. I am the *only* one being a loyal friend to him.'

'God, don't tell me you had something to do with him getting stuck up that tree yesterday. He told me about it. No, there's no way . . .'

'He must never know, Jack. Never, ever, ever. And you mustn't tell Chloe or Rani either. No one must ever know. I was simply trying to help him out by making him look a hero, and it went wrong, OK?'

'I'll say it went wrong! What were you *thinking*, Carrie? You're mad. You're madder than Minnie the Mad of Mad Town.'

'I was trying to be a good friend to Tom! That's what I was thinking! And I seem to be the only person who wants to be that at the moment.'

Jack's voice became gentle. 'Carrie, we're all upset about Tom and Chloe, you know. We all care about both of them. But we can't do anything about what's happened. It's out of our hands.'

'You see! That's just that kind of defeatist attitude I'm fighting against.'

Jack sighed and changed the subject. 'OK. Shall we meet tomorrow, then? We can talk some more. After the drama course, in the Coffee Bean?'

So heaven, heaven, heaven, all is well with Jack and I am seeing him tomorrow. We will talk about everything and he will make it all seem all right. I want everybody in the whole wide world to have a boyfriend like him. Why why why do some people want to change and upset everything?

I am off to shave my legs and paint my toenails pink.

## 9.30 p.m.

I was lying on my bed this afternoon (where else would I be as I am a prisoner in my own home) wearing my oldest shorts and my red T-shirt, twiddling my toes in the air to dry the nail polish. I could hear Dad mowing the lawn. Mum was asleep on a lounger on the patio, and Ned was still out skateboarding. The doorbell went. I waited. Surely someone else would hear it. But no. It rang again. I have to do everything in this house. I am basically the maid. I sighed in the direction of my toes, lowered them, and swung my feet carefully on to the floor.

Gregg Madison was standing on my doorstep. I looked over his shoulder into the road, and saw Mona tapping the steering wheel of the car, engine running. He was holding out a bag of books.

'I wanted to give these back to you. We've just got back from London. Gus tells me the woman at the library was pretty fierce on getting books back on time and I wasn't sure when I'd get another opportunity. Thanks so much for getting them out Carrie, they were great. Meant that when the writers were in the read-through, I knew what everyone was talking about! And I didn't come across as completely dumb.'

I couldn't help smiling. He didn't seem like he was acting nice. He *was* nice. He really wasn't stuck-up or starry at all.

But he's not Tom! I gave myself a shake. Tom's my friend and I wouldn't give up on him. I would be loyal.

'Thanks,' I said, taking them from him. There was an awkward silence.

'Could I ask you something?' he said.

'OK,' I answered cautiously.

'Erm, you don't happen to know if Chloe got that letter I told you about do you?'

'Yes. Yes she did,' I said crisply.

'And she read it?'

'She read it.'

'It's just, I was an idiot and forgot to put down my mobile number . . . So I don't know, er, what her, um . . . response was.'

I stared blankly back at him. The neighbour's dog barked and I heard an ice-cream van chiming in the distance.

He seemed to slump down in front of me. 'Guess not so good,

then.' He sighed before saying, 'Look, I need Chloe to know something important. We did a lot of publicity in London and Mona wanted me to be photographed all over town with Paige Tennessee, you know, my co-star in the movie?'

I nodded. Her blue eyes, blond hair and perfect smile were always in the gossip pages.

'I want Chloe to know that that's *all* it was . . .' he went on. 'Publicity. There's nothing going on there. Mona says stories about stars being together gets great press for movies, so I've gone along with it. Chloe needs to know that I've made it clear to Paige that that's all it is too – whatever Paige says to the press. She's really loving telling all the reporters that we're an item. But it's just not true. You will tell Chloe, won't you? Because she's going to see it in all the papers and magazines – it was in some today and will be in more tomorrow – and I wouldn't want her to think . . . Well, you will tell her, won't you?'

I nodded again. Nodding is not the same as *saying*.

*Saying* 'yes' would be lying.

He looked hard at me. I said nothing. I could see hurt starting to cloud the clear blue of his eyes.

'I'm guessing from your face that she's decided to stay with Tom, then?'

I just stood there.

Gregg would get over it. He was a famous TV star. He'd be over it in a *minute*.

Someone *had* to help Tom. And stop Chloe from drifting away from us.

Eventually he nodded. 'I see. OK.' He ran his hands through his blond hair and managed to force a smile. 'You can't say I didn't try. At least I know there's no point in staying . . .' He looked at me. 'Well, never mind now . . .'

Mona beeped the horn loudly and we both jumped.

Gregg began to walk backwards down the garden path. 'Tell her anyway about the Paige Tennessee thing. I don't want her to ever think I lied to her. I mean, I really need her to know I meant every word I ever said to her . . .'

He tumbled into the waiting car and I watched it disappear down the road. And I thought, *What have I done?*

 RANI'S TIP: • • • • • • • • • • • • • • • • • •

For well-painted nails, always give the bottle a good shake first. Wipe the excess off the brush, then place one stroke down the middle of a nail. Apply a second stroke on one side of it, then a third on the other side. Wait for that to dry before applying a another coat, and when that's dry, apply a clear top coat to protect your hard work. Waving your hands like a crazy thing to dry the nails is more effective than blowing on them - the moisture in your breath actually makes the polish take longer to dry.

# Chapter 15

## Monday 7.00 a.m.

Rani rang last night to see if I was feeling better. I felt bad about lying to her earlier about being ill. But then again, I was feeling bad about a lot of things.

I realised immediately that Rani was low.

'What's the matter?' I asked her.

'I upset Chloe. I didn't mean to. I meant to cheer her up.'

I could certainly relate to that.

'What happened?' I asked.

'I don't know if I want to tell you.'

'Why not?'

'Because you'll go all funny and jump down the phone at me.'

'I won't! I promise.'

'Even if it's about Gregg?' Rani went on cautiously.

'What about him?' I felt my face go red with guilt and my heart started to beat rather fast, even though there was no one there to see me.

'You know, well you *don't*, because Chloe wouldn't tell you, but *I'll* tell you: ever since Gregg left for London she's been a nervous wreck waiting for him to get back. I mean *literally* living to see him again. She says she's known since the first moment she spoke to him she felt something special about him . . .'

'Mmm.' I was hating this conversation. And myself.

'She didn't want to cause Tom any embarrassment yesterday and that's why we left before he'd got down from the tree. Actually, she thought it was incredibly brave of him to climb up when she knew he was so scared of heights. She said he was quite the hero, if a bit misguided . . . I went with her because I know she's in such a state waiting for Gregg to get back. So to cheer her up, I popped into the newsagents round the corner from her place and bought some chocolate and some celebrity mags.' I heard Rani groan down the phone. 'If only I'd known . . .'

My heart was really thumping now. 'Known what?'

'They were full of pictures of Gregg and Paige Tennessee! Apparently they're an item. Interviews with Paige about how happy they were and everything. You were right all along, Carrie. And only a few days ago he was writing Chloe romantic letters and seemed so genuine. I mean, I know he's an actor, but honestly! He had us all fooled, except you. You were the *only* one who saw him for what he really was. Chloe is absolutely devastated. And I mean heartbroken. I've never seen her like this. Ever.

'God, that's awful,' I said. And I meant it. 'You don't think she'd go back with . . .' I ventured tentatively.

'You must be joking! No, Carrie! How many times do I have to say it? She's kind of busy dealing with the pain of knowing that someone she trusted has made a complete fool of her. She says she can't bear the thought that everything he said was a lie. Not a word of truth. That she could have actually believed that she was different from all the other girls who crowd around him? She feels so stupid.'

'Perhaps . . . perhaps there is an explanation.'

'Explanation! Gregg coming out of every nightclub in London with Paige on his arm. I think it was clear! And anyway we know he's back at Maddy's now. My mum saw their car, you know the one they drive around in these days, with the driver and the tinted windows, and he hasn't been to see her. No. He's dropped Chloe like a stone . . . You were so right. He was Her Hideous Mistake.'

'I don't know . . .'

'Got to go now, Mum's calling me,' Rani cried. 'I'll see you tomorrow for pumpkin painting, OK?'

'Wait! I've got something to say . . .' I said feebly. But she was gone.

And that was that.

No wonder I haven't slept all night.

The bellowing has begun in the shower so that means it's time to get up. Thank goodness.

I have something very important to do.


## 6.00 p.m.

I wanted desperately to talk to Rani on the way to the village hall, but Talullah was full of her plans for her birthday sleepover and I couldn't get a word in.

'Mum says I can have one, it's going to be brilliant. We're going to try on each others' clothes, do our hair and make-up, watch DVDs and eat pizza and loads of chocolate and marshmallows . . .'

'Sounds excellent.' Rani smiled. 'Can I come?'

'Wow! That would be . . .' and then Talullah realised Rani was joking.

'Stop teasing!' she giggled. 'It's going to be great.'

'Who *are* you inviting?' I asked.

'Florence, *obviously*. And all the other Year Six girls on the course. And Jeremy. Not the pony girls, they're off on a pony club weekend, but all the rest. I want to have them over before I start at Boughton. Mum agrees it would be a good idea.'

Rani and I looked at each other.

'*All* the girls?' Rani asked.

Talullah frowned. 'Yes. I know what you're thinking, but I *am* going to invite Donna and Shanaid. I've been trying hard not to fight with them, but it's not getting us anywhere. Besides, *I* would never leave anyone out. Whoever they may be. That's acting like them and I don't want to do that. I won't be mean.'

'Well, good for you,' I said and caught Rani's eye again. I hoped Talullah's optimistic plans for her sleepover party weren't going to be cruelly dashed. When we arrived, Talullah rushed in and I grabbed Rani's arm and held her back. 'I absolutely have to talk to Chloe this morning. It's super, super important.'

'Whoooh. OK,' Rani replied. 'That sounds serious. But we're late, so tell me about it inside.'

But when we went in and looked around the hall, not only was Chloe nowhere to be seen but Miss Lamb swept over and grabbed us. She'd given herself a bit of make-over at the weekend. The long grey plait had gone and she had a new shorter, styled hair cut. It really suited her. I noticed Mr Hopper had bought himself a new jacket last week as well. Miss Lamb didn't give us a moment to talk.

'Come on, girls! Chloe's not coming in this morning, apparently she's not feeling too good, and I've got to rehearse the little ones and there's Cinderella's ball dress to finish. Could you help out with the dress, Carrie? And Rani, can you come and help me with the mice? They're simply not getting their scampering right at all . . .'

Rani grinned at me and scampered off behind Miss Lamb, with her hands up in front of her like little mice paws.

I spent the morning taking up Cinderella's ballgown. One of the mice had donated her big sister's bridesmaid dress. It was cream silk and Chloe had already stuck tiny diamanté drops all over it and added glittery gold bows at the hem and the neckline and a long sash at the back. Talullah was in a good mood. She had been very clever and invited Emma, April, Prema, Jeremy and Nicki to her party one by one as they had come into the hall. They had all said a cautious yes. By the time Donna and Shanaid arrived Talullah was already standing on a table and I was pinning up her hem. I spotted Donna staring at Talullah and I could see the envious look in her eyes. It didn't bode well for how *she* was going to reply to her invite, but I had troubles enough of my own to worry about. I desperately, urgently needed to talk to Chloe. As soon as possible. I had to tell her what Gregg had told me. Now I realised I was going to have to do it by phone as soon as I got out of the hall, which wasn't the way I'd wanted to do it, but I knew it couldn't wait a moment longer.

So I was thrilled when Rani and I came out at the end of the morning and Chloe was standing by the gate.

'Chloe! I'm so glad to see you! I need to talk to you . . .' I hurtled towards her but I stopped short when I got close enough to see the expression on her face.

She was white with anger.

'Chloe, this is so important. You must listen to me . . .' I began.

'*Listen* to you! Listen to you!' She was shaking with emotion. 'You've got to be joking! You've wrecked my life! Deliberately! I thought you were one of my best friends. What did I *ever* do to you that you could hate me so much, Carrie?'

'I don't hate you, Chloe! What are you talking about?'

'What on earth is going on?' Rani was standing next to us now, and behind her a curious crowd was gathering.

Chloe turned to her. 'After seeing those pictures in those magazines yesterday, you know how upset I was? I know it was a terrible idea, but I wanted to try and see Gregg, one last time, get some kind of explanation or apology or something.' She saw Rani's expression. '*Yes.* I know it was a crazy idea. But this morning I went to Maddy's house and waited at the gates, just like all the other hopeful fans that hang around there all the time now. I was hoping to catch his car. And a car did come through. But Gregg wasn't in it, it was Mona, surrounded by her bags. She saw me, wound her window down and told me the Madisons have all left for London. And she was *so* glad that I had realised that I couldn't possibly have a future with Gregg and had decided to stay with my *local* boyfriend . . .'

'But I don't understand,' Rani frowned. 'What would make her think that you had decided to stay with Tom? And what's it got to do with Carrie, anyway?'

Chloe's eyes flashed. 'I'll tell you what it's got to do with her. Yesterday Mona took Gregg round to Carrie's to return some books. What did Mona say exactly?' Chloe put on Mona's

American accent. 'Gregg was pretty cut up after talking to your friend, honey, but I want you to know that *I'm* sure you've made the right decision. I know Gregg wanted to tell your friend the Paige thing had been just for publicity – he was so jumpy about it the whole London trip – and I'm sure your friend went and told *you*. But I'm glad you've seen sense, Chloe, and realised that you and Gregg can't have any kind of future. So maybe now the Paige thing *won't* be just for publicity after all?' Chloe clenched her fists, and went on. 'She gave me a horrible smile, I began to talk, to tell her I didn't know what she was talking about . . . but she wound up the window and drove off.'

Chloe stopped and stared directly at me. 'And you didn't tell me what he said about Paige did you, Carrie? Instead you told him that I wasn't interested, didn't you? You didn't let him know that I'd finished with Tom, did you? You let him believe that I'd chosen Tom and not him.'

Rani looked at me. 'Carrie, you *wouldn't* have? You didn't?'

'I know I should never have done it, Chloe. You have no idea . . . I'm so, so, sorry. I made the biggest mistake —'

'Really?' Chloe snapped. 'I thought you said it was *me* who was making the mistake . . .'

'I promise you, as soon as he left I felt awful, I wanted to tell you first thing this morning, I said to Rani —'

'Oh right, so now you know I've found out, *NOW* you say were going to tell me. Well, do you know something, Carrie? I don't believe you. Because basically this has all been about how *you* feel. And what *you* wanted. Not about anyone else . . .'

'I didn't —'

'Well, Gregg's gone London now, no doubt straight into the arms of Paige, and even though I tried to tell Mona she'd got it all wrong, she's never going to tell him, is she? I'm never, ever going to get another chance with him again.'

Chloe burst into tears.

'Chloe, please don't cry. As soon as I'd done it I knew it was wrong. I should have called you straight away, but I didn't know they were planning to leave.'

'Well, it's a bit late now, isn't it? Because he *is* in London. And the publicity machine is going to get into full swing and no one's going to be able to get near him!'

I was horrified. 'Chloe, I've been such a fool. I am so, so sorry.' I moved towards her, but she pushed me back.

'Get away from me! I never want to see you or speak to you again!'

She turned and began to run down the road, sobbing. Rani went after her.

I felt the tears begin to roll down my cheeks. A hand slipped into mine. 'Come on, Carrie. Come with me, my mum will give you a lift.' And I slipped through a huddle of staring onlookers and gratefully sank into the back of Mrs Banks' car.

Anyone can look like they belong in Hollywood, but you've got find the clothes that really suit you, not just whatever is in fashion. True style is about making the most of yourself, so consult your friends about what you look best in, or ask in places that offer free personal shoppers for their professional opinion.

# Chapter 16

Tuesday 8.00 p.m.

I am writing this on the table at the bottom of the garden. Alone. Which is something I had better get used to, as I have not a single friend left in the world.

Mrs Banks dropped me off a couple of bus stops away from town and, after thanking her and Talullah many times, I went to meet Jack in the Coffee Bean.

Where I thought I'd at least be with *someone* who cared about me and didn't think I was a vile, wicked person.

But Tom was there. And Jack gave me a 'He was really low – what could I do?' look. Which I totally understood. But it meant I couldn't talk about what had just happened, even though it was obvious I wasn't quite on my usual sparkling form. In fact, I was pretty much a black hole of gloom, even though I tried to be cheerful for Tom's sake by doing an impression of Donna trying not to explode with jealousy over Cinderella's ballgown.

'Talullah sounds like she can cope with most of what life throws at her.' Jack smiled.

'I know, she's a toughie. She's so brave, you should see her climbing that tree . . .'

And I stopped. Too late. Tom was straight on to me.

'What do you mean, "You should see her climbing that tree"?'

'Nothing. I mean, she was brave to think she *could* do it, but she couldn't, could she? As you know.' I gave a little cough.

But Tom was frowning now. 'I always thought it was odd that she was down that tree in minutes . . . Carrie . . .' He looked up. 'Was that all some kind of deliberate plan?'

'No!' I shrieked. 'No.' And then I looked at Tom's face and knew I couldn't cope with lying to anyone ever again from now on. 'Yes.' I sighed. 'OK, yes. I'm sorry. I thought it might make you look good. You know, with Chloe . . .'

'You did *what*? And what could *possibly* be good about her seeing me lifted out of a tree by a fireman like a stuck kitten?'

'Hardly a kitten . . .' Jack said, looking at Tom's stocky form, but he wasn't listening.

Tom got up. 'How *could* you *do* that to me?'

'I was trying to help you!' I cried.

'REALLY? To help? Well, if that's your idea of help, please don't bother! Keep out of my life. Got that?'

I hung my head. 'Yes.'

'I'm going off for a walk now.' And he got up and started heading for the door.

'You better go after him, Jack,' I said. 'I think he really deserves to be with a good friend now.'

Jack put his arm around my shoulder. 'But what about you?' he asked. 'Seems like you're not feeling so great yourself.'

I shook my head. 'I'll be fine. I've got loads of stuff I need to do at home – sequins to sew on ballgowns. You know how it is.'

Jack looked at me seriously. 'Carrie . . . About the Tom thing?'

And suddenly the awfulness of everything came tumbling

down on me and the worst part of it was I had no one to blame but myself. I didn't *deserve* friends. 'Don't say it!' I yelled, putting my hand over my ears. 'I know you think I'm awful and the worst thing is, you don't even know the whole story! I know you're going to hate me just like the others do when you hear it. I know you will! So we might as well end it now. So go! Go and be with someone who deserves your sympathy. Go and be with someone who deserves you being kind to them.'

Jack hesitated, shocked.

'Go on!' I cried, pushing him out of the seat. 'I really, really, want you to go!'

And I gave him a huge shove.

'What is the matter with you?!' he said.

'Go!'

So he did. After his good friend.

I've lost all mine.

I wished Talullah better luck than me.

She had asked Donna and Shanaid to her sleepover at the end of this morning. As they were never apart she had had to ask them both at the same time. They had looked at her in total astonishment.

'The others say they think they might make it,' Talullah offered in response to their silence.

Donna's eyes narrowed. 'Really?' she said dangerously. 'They didn't mention it.' Then she inspected her nails for a while, glanced up again and said, 'I'll have to check my diary. I must say I'm surprised the others said yes straight away, without . . . er, checking theirs. What about you, Shanaid?'

'I'll have to check mine too.'

No need to check my diary.

Rani didn't turn up on the walk to the hall with Talullah and me this morning. I saw her talking to Chloe when I arrived. I ducked my head down and went round the back of the stage and painted the coach on my own. No one came to join me.

I wasn't expecting them to.

No. My diary is empty. Empty of friends. Empty of my lovely friends – for the rest of my life. Mum has just brought me a cup of tea and a piece of toast. Sure sign I am not keeping my feelings secret enough and her misery radar is beeping. I cannot tell her what has happened, though. I'm too ashamed.

### Wednesday 6.00 p.m.

Cocoa and chocolate biscuits from Mum. She looks worried. Ned has got wind of what's happened. One of his skateboarding mates has a little sister who is one of the mice. Thank you, Ned. I will remember that. I still cannot talk about it. I have kept my phone switched off. No one is going to ring me anyway. All my girl friends hate me. Tom hates me and now that Jack surely knows the whole story, he will hate me too.

Talullah is about the only person in the world who doesn't hate me. She was very upset today. She told me on the way in that all the others who had said that they *would* come to her party had come back to her and said they weren't so sure they could make it now . . .

I could tell that she was trying to not to show she cared.

'So it will just be me and Florence, and that's great. I know we can have fun just the two of us. But we're not really the experts on make-up or clothes . . .'

'I'll come and help do you a makeover,' I said suddenly. Why not? Florence and Talullah were great girls. Why shouldn't I help them out if I could?

'Would you?!' Talullah gasped. 'That would be so brilliant! You wouldn't have to actually sleep on the floor of my room with Florence and me . . .' She flushed. 'Seeing as you live opposite. Unless you wanted to . . .?'

'Er, no. I think I'll just pop off home when it gets late,' I said quickly.

She clapped her hands and gave a little skip. 'I'd *love* to tell all the others that you're coming . . .' She frowned. 'But I'm not going to. I don't want them to come just because you're going to be there. Doing makeovers . . .'

'Absolutely!' I agreed, touched that she thought it would make a difference. 'And don't get too excited, I'm not that brilliant at them. It's really Chloe and Rani who are the experts in that department . . .'

And I remembered all the sleepovers that we had had over the years and all the laughing and fun and I suddenly felt tears prick my eyes. I changed the subject.

### 6.30 p.m.

Mum just came in with more cocoa and said three things:

    1. Jack keeps calling on the land line and why won't I speak to him?

    2. Have I seen all the publicity about the new Brad Pitt movie

premiere in London this Saturday night? Gregg is sure to be there with that stunning actress he's dating now.

3. Was I looking forward to Moulton Fair this weekend? Especially as Maddy will be back. How lovely to have all your friends together again.

I know she was only trying to cheer me up with the last one. But I burst into tears.

 MADDY'S TIP: • • • • • • • • • • • • • • • • • • • •
If you think you're not very photogenic, even after you've gotten all dressed up, there are a few things you can do to help in front of the camera. Try standing slightly side on and turn towards the camera to look slimmer, or put a hand on your hip to prevent squashed-looking arms. And most importantly – SMILE! No amount of make-up can compete with someone who really looks like they are having fun.

# Chapter 17

Thursday 7.30 p.m.

I felt a bit better after telling Mum.

She listened very carefully to the whole story and then she said, 'I can see that you've learned a big lesson, Carrie. And I can see it's a very hard one but you must realise that some things have to change. However much we like the way things are, some things aren't going to stay the same. And boyfriends are one of the most changeable things of all. Chloe can't stay with Tom to please you. You know that's silly. She is on her own journey through her life and she has to move on.'

'But I don't *want* her to move on. If she stays with Tom everything will be the same. But it won't be if she's with Gregg. It will all go wrong between us,' I wailed.

'But why? Why are you scared about Chloe seeing Gregg?' Mum asked.

'I'm scared she'll . . . I don't know . . . leave us behind . . . I'm scared . . .' – I put my head in my hands – 'that she'll move on and get all glamorous and famous and forget all about us.'

And then Mum laughed. Which I thought was pretty heartless and definitely something to tell future therapist Dr Jennings, but she stopped as soon as she saw my face and went on.

'Forget you! Carrie, for goodness' sake – firstly, you've all been friends since you were little girls, she's not going to let all that history disappear, and secondly, you're not really the kind of character that people forget very easily . . .' She frowned. 'Actually, you are being very insulting to Chloe thinking she might be that shallow . . .'

'Well, it's too late now, isn't it?' I wailed. 'Through trying to keep my friends I've managed to lose all of them.'

'I'm sure you haven't,' she said in that way mums do when they have no idea of how horrendous things really are, even though you have just explained it to them QUITE CLEARLY.

She handed me a tissue.

'Mum,' I sniffed quite a while later.

'What?'

'I've thought of a plan . . .'

## Friday 7.00 p.m.

It took all my persuasive powers, but in the end Mum said yes but on one condition: I have to bring her a cup of tea in bed every morning as long as I live at home.

I pointed out that this blatant slavery didn't fit in with the talk we had just had about people having personal freedom but she said that was different – but I can't see how.

Anyway, I feel it will be worth it in the end.

Spent another morning hiding around the back of the stage. The others were all putting the finishing touches to costumes for the final dress rehearsal later on. I couldn't bear to go into the hall and watch it, not with Rani and Chloe looking at me accusingly so I said I had to go early, slipped out the back and missed it.

Mum held out the phone to me as I walked in the door. 'I don't want —' I started.

'It's Jackie,' she said. I reluctantly took the phone.

'A little bird told me that you might be free for the Alton Towers trip after all?' she trilled.

I thought about it for about ten seconds.

I could go. I could go and pretend I was fine, that I was having a great time hanging out with my new friends . . . And then an image of me throwing my head back, fake laughing as I plunged to certain death on a roller coaster with Jackie and the others shrieking 'Exterminate! Exterminate!' flashed through my mind.

I know I am through with pretending.

'I'm afraid I can't.'

'But why?' Jackie pressed.

I winced. It was like a knife turning in my heart.

'I've got a lot of stuff to finish off, Jackie. The stage is up on Moulton field, and there's all the scenery and props for the show to get ready over there. I just can't spare the time.'

'Well, OK, then,' Jackie sighed. 'Shame you'll miss all the fun tomorrow.'

'Mmm,' I answered. I didn't deserve any fun. And it wouldn't be without my best friends.

I was pleased that I'd be occupied tomorrow. It would make the day go faster because I was going to be very busy indeed in the evening.

Mum is yelling up the stairs. I *thought* I heard the house phone ringing. She says if I don't switch my mobile on again she will go mental. Better go.

It was Talullah. In floods of tears. I went straight round. Her mum answered the door looking anxious and immediately directed me upstairs.

'Tell her it's going to have be cut out, Carrie. There's no other way . . .'

Lying on her bed, with Florence kneeling beside it, was a sobbing figure.

'What on earth is going on?' I asked, shocked. It was so unlike Talullah to cry. And what was that on her head?

Florence bit her lip. 'It happened at the dress rehearsal. We were getting our costumes ready and some of the glass jewels on Talullah's tiara had fallen off. Donna said some had come off her coat for the ball scene as well and she offered to stick them back on. Only problem was she was sticking hers on to thick material and Talalluh's on to a tiara, with holes in it. And Donna used the super-glue from Mr Hopper's tool box. She said she was fed up with them falling off with the school glue that we normally use . . .'

'So,' I sighed, 'let me guess . . .'

Florence nodded. 'So when Talullah put her tiara on for the ball scene it hadn't dried yet and got stuck in her hair. She can't get it out.' Florence lowered her voice. 'Not without scissors . . .'

'Nooooo! Don't say scissors . . .' A howl went up from the bed. 'I won't let *anyone* cut my hair.'

Talullah sat up and it could not be denied she had a tiara stuck firmly in the spirals and corkscrews. She began tugging at it ferociously.

'Stop it!' Florence begged. She turned to me again. 'We all

begged her to stop pulling at it. Emma, April, Jeremy, Prema, Nicki, even Shanaid. It was horrible.'

'What did Donna do?' I asked.

'She tried to make out that it was funny at first, but she soon realised that it wasn't. But by the time she realised how serious it was, none of the others would really look at her. I think they were all shocked. I don't know if she did it on purpose or not, I can't believe she would, but to even think for one second that it might it be funny . . .'

'It's the worst thing that's ever happened to me in my *life* . . .' Talullah wailed. 'I'll be the ugliest Cinderella in the world and everyone will laugh at me . . . and I got that glue all over the dress as well – when I was trying to wipe it off my hands. I'm not going to do the show. I can't! And I can't have my hair cut anyway – Mum's tried the local salons and no one's got an appointment at the weekends.'

I knelt down next to Florence. 'Look, Talullah. Fact one: You *are* going to be Cinderella on Sunday and you are going to look stunning. I will make sure of it. You are an actor and actors don't let the show down. Or Miss Lamb, who's worked so hard on this.

Fact two: You cannot go around with a tiara stuck on your head all your life.

Fact three: You *are* going to have to let someone cut your hair . . .'

Talullah broke into fresh wails.

'Now listen to me,' I went on. 'I am going to tell you something that Rani's mum told me that is very, very true. There is no girl in the whole wide world who has not, or who *will* not, one day in the future, have a bad hair day. Ask Chloe. When she was your age she went to the hairdressers and told them she wanted it slightly shorter and she came out with six inches lopped off. She cried for days and kept the hair in a shoe box. Every time she opened it, she cried some more.'

'And this is supposed to be making me feel better how?' Talullah queried. Her mum had arrived at the door and was looking at me curiously.

'Because look at her now! And you never saw *me* when my home bleaching went wrong and I looked like some orange stripey mutant tiger girl. You see, look at us now, we're fine. I'm going to call Rani's mum and see if she will help you. She's brilliant. She used to be a hairdresser and sorted me out that time. You'll go to Rani's house and she'll give you magazines and cups of tea like in a salon and she'll make you look fantastic. And the one heavenly, marvellous thing about hair, that every girl needs to remember, is that it *grows*. Yours will grow back in a flash, and who knows? You may not want it longer again, not after you've seen how cool you're going to look with it in a different style.'

Talullah put her legs over the side of her bed and blew her nose into tissue. 'Do you think so?'

'I know so. Look, I'm going to phone Rani's mum now.'

And I did, with crossed fingers, and for once fate wasn't against me. Rani's mum answered the phone.

**CARRIE'S TIP:** • • • • • • • • • • • • • • • • • • • • •

Talking a problem through with people is usually a good thing, and sometimes that can mean talking to a parent. As is clearly shown in their general lifestyle, they have a totally different perspective on things, and occasionally, that can be quite useful.

# Chapter 18

*Saturday 5.00 p.m.*

Mum says we need to be ready to set off in half an hour. I have butterflies in my stomach. I hope I'm not making the most terrible mistake.

I will take some deep breaths, shower and change. That will calm me down. And *cool* me down – it's a scorching day today.

Miss Lamb and I loaded up the scenery and props this morning and put the first load in the car. To my surprise Mr Hopper suddenly appeared looking very dapper in clean shirt and cords.

'Thought I'd better come and see if you needed a bit of muscle.' He smiled. I caught Miss Lamb blushing.

After we had taken the first load to the stage that Tom and his dad had helped build, I said I'd stay and sort out the scenery while they went back for more.

I'm even a gooseberry to old people now.

Once they had gone I had the place to myself. The field was peaceful and deserted in the morning sunlight. I began to edge a large wooden tree into position. I found my mind wandering, thinking about Tom, Rani and Chloe, and now Maddy would be back . . . and of course I thought about —

'Hello.'

I jumped, screamed, and dropped the tree with a loud crash.

'Great.' Jack grinned, leaning against a wooden post on the other side of the stage. 'First you won't answer my calls and now you're attacking me with ye olde English oak trees.'

I stared at him. I couldn't help it. My heart soared. I was *so* pleased to see him. But I pulled myself together.

'Did the others tell you what I did?'

'Yes.'

'So why are you here, then?'

'Because I wanted to see you. Your mobile is permanently off and your mum says you won't come to the phone. We had a kind of boyfriend–girlfriend thing going on for a while. I liked it. I'd like some more of it please.'

I stayed on the other side of the stage.

'Even though you know your girlfriend lied to two of her best friends and may have ruined their lives?'

'Even so.'

'That makes me not a very nice person, you know. And anyway, you said you hated liars, and I lied. Well, I didn't tell the truth but that amounts to the same thing.'

'You were wrong not to tell Chloe about what Gregg said – but I totally believe you were going to. I know you, you couldn't have lived with yourself.'

'I know! I felt terrible. I will never interfere with people's love-lives again!'

Jack frowned. 'You're being very hard on yourself.'

'Well, I've lost all my friends and it serves me right,' I added.

'Not all your friends . . .' Jack stepped across the stage towards me. 'You've still got me.' He took my hands and held them in front of me.

'Do you think I'll ever be able to make up with them?' I asked.

He put his arms around me. 'Look, Carrie, they know you as well as I do, maybe better. Rani and Chloe have known you forever. You love your friends. Maybe a bit too much at times. And that's what's caused all this. Not because you didn't like them, but because you feel about them so strongly. You didn't want anything to happen that made you think that you might lose them. But I'd say you've really suffered about what you've done. You've certainly learned your lesson. Tom understands, we've talked and he can see that, in your crazy way, you were doing it because you cared. He's gone away for a couple of days to stay with some cousins. He's going to call you. Maybe the others will also understand, given time.'

'I know that I was ridiculous now.' I leaned into his shoulder. 'But look at all the damage I've caused. I can't see that they will ever forgive me. Not now.'

'Well, there's nothing you can do about it. Time will sort this out, Carrie, you'll see.'

And he kissed me and it felt so good to be back in his arms again and know that *someone* cared.

And he was right. Time may sort it out. But perhaps I can help it along. I didn't tell Jack my new plan – I just didn't want him to make me change my mind.

I'd better get ready. Mum is doing me a big favour and I don't want to keep her waiting.

Which reminds me, I must find my lucky Union Jack pants.

RANI'S TIP: • • • • • • • • • • • • • • • • • • • •

Sometimes even making yourself over doesn't help you feel better about yourself. At times like these, it's a good idea just to find your own space for a bit so you can think about things.

# Chapter 19

## Sunday 7.00 a.m.

I know I'm exhausted, but it's Moulton Fair today and there's loads to do. I've also got to get my make-up and hair stuff ready for Talullah's sleepover.

Which proves you *can* be busy without your best friends around. But it isn't the same. It's not the same at all. And even though having Jack as a boyfriend is lovely, it's not like being friends with Chloe, Rani and Maddy.

I miss them.

I miss them *so* much.

And I have no idea if my plan worked last night. Though I know I did all I could. What happens now is out of my hands.

I have to call Maddy this morning. I have a favour to ask her. And as it's not actually for *me*, I'm hoping she'll say yes and won't slam the phone down on me. I keep thinking of them all laughing their heads off and having a brilliant time together. Without me.

I bet they're having the best time ever.

The house is very quiet. Mum must be tired after all the excitement and driving last night.

## 5.00 p.m.

The first thing I did when I left the house was cross the road and go and see how Talullah was.

She opened the door to me.

'Wow!' I gasped. 'You look fantastic!'

And she did. Rani's mum had done a brilliant job and her new funky short hair suited Talullah's pretty, animated face. Mrs Banks came into the hall, looking relieved and happy.

'Thanks.' Talullah beamed. 'I mean it, really, thanks for everything. You were great yesterday. You are still coming tonight, aren't you?'

'Of course!' I cried. 'Wouldn't miss it for the world.'

'I know it's just going to be you, me and Florence . . .'

'Hey!' I interrupted. 'With that crowd coming, who needs anyone else?'

She smiled again. 'Pity about the dress, isn't it? Now my hair is so nice?'

'Yes, well,' I said, 'you never know, something might turn up . . . I'll see you later.'

When I got to the field it was already a buzz of activity. The bunting was up and the stalls were being set out: coconut shies, plastic ducks in paddling pools, shooting ranges, face painting, cakes, jams, pies, vegetables, flowers, not to mention the roundabout, helter skelter and bouncy castle. I could already smell the candy floss, toffee apples and the frying onions on Mr Hopper's hot dog stand.

This would normally have filled me with a wonderful sense of happiness, but then a day like this would be a day I would normally spend with my friends. We would have enjoyed looking out for hot looks between Miss Lamb and Mr Hopper over the sizzling sausages, watching the mice trying to upstage each other in the show, cheering Talullah and Florence and all the others on . . . But after all my effort last night, there was no sign that it had had any effect.

So I took up residence in my new home these days: at the back of the stage, and quietly got on with getting some screens up on the grass, to make a place for changing costumes.

'Carrie! Carrie! Where are you?' It was a distinctive American accent. Maddy! When I had phoned her earlier, her mother had answered and so I'd spoken to her instead. It had been a bit of a relief, to be honest. But now Maddy was on the field and calling me and I was just going to *have* to answer when I heard Miss Lamb say, 'Can't you find her? Can I help instead?' And I was spared.

The field began to fill up and I watched everyone arrive. Including Jack, who came round the back of the stage to keep me company in my hiding place. Well, I say everyone arrived – almost everyone. One girl hadn't turned up. I dared to look up over the stage making sure my head was hidden from the audience behind ye olde English oak. The rows of chairs put out in front of the stage were already full and people were standing and sitting on the grass all around. To my horror I spotted Chloe, Rani and Maddy walking around the side of the audience and heading my way.

As I feared, they appeared around the back of the stage. I turned to Jack and he shrugged his shoulders. I was going to have to face them, but before they could say a word, Miss Lamb ran into the middle of us, scarf awry and her face in an agonised expression.

'Have any of you seen her? What are we going to do? We have no Prince Charming. Has *anyone* seen Donna?'

We all shook our heads. I was trying to hide behind Miss Lamb's large bulk.

'But it's a DISASTER!' she wailed. 'Anyone could wing it on the talking parts, but no one else knows the words to the songs, the duets . . .'

'You could do it.'

We all turned round to see a smiling Mr Hopper. 'You know them . . .'

Miss Lamb blushed. 'Well, that's, er, very kind of you, Donald, but even I know that *visually* I am not what our younger audience will be looking for.'

Mr Hopper looked like he disagreed, but the rest of us knew Miss Lamb had a point. 'After all the hard work everyone's put into it, it's just TOO bad. It's just so, so *disappointing* . . . I know it's just a little local show, but it means a lot to me to do it well. That dreadful woman from Pitsford will get to crow again . . .' Miss Lamb sat down heavily on Cinderella's kitchen table and sighed.

'Can I help?'

My heart lifted. Chloe spun round and gasped.

Standing there, looking impossibly gorgeous as ever, was Gregg Madison.

'Gregg!' she whispered. 'What are you doing here!'

'A friend of yours, er . . . found me in London.' He gave me a big grin. 'She gave me a letter that explained some things.'

They were now looking at each other as if they were never going to stop.

'And look, Chloe, I know it's not fair to ask you if you'd give someone with a mad career like mine a chance . . .'

'It is! It is!' she yelled and jumped straight into his arms. He spun her round and then they kissed like they were never going to stop that either.

'Plenty of time for that later!' Miss Lamb boomed, beaming from ear to ear. 'We've got a show to put on.'

And it was a terrific show. The audience went bananas when Gregg came out as Prince Charming. He must be one of the few boys in the world who could improvise well enough and make working alongside a bunch of primary kids look like the coolest thing in the world. For Talullah it was a dream come true. With the stunning diamanté tiara and beaded Chanel dress that Maddy had lent her, she looked adorable. Florence, who had started out on the course barely being able to be heard further than the first row, acted and sung her socks off. I could see her mother in the audience, bursting with pride. But the most important thing was everyone – the mice, the ugly sisters, *everyone* – had a great time.

And it was so good to see Chloe smiling and laughing her head off. The happiest I'd ever seen her. And I know Gregg was singing all the love songs for her. At least I'd managed to get something right.

I felt someone's arms going around me.

'Feeling better now?'

'Yes. Thanks, Jack.'

'Staying for a while?'

I looked at everyone and shook my head. 'No, everyone's so happy now and it might make it awkward if I hang around. And I've got a sleepover party to go to tonight.'

He kissed me for a long time. 'See you tomorrow, then.' He

brushed a lock of hair out of my eyes. 'Have fun . . . and hey . . .'
he caught my hand as I slipped out of his arms, his dark eyes
suddenly serious, 'you won't go changing *your* mind about
anything too soon, will you?'

'I won't,' I said, blushing. 'I feel you and me, well . . . we've
only just begun . . .'

'Me too,' he replied and pulled me back to kiss me again.

 CHLOE'S TIP: •••••••••••••••••••••
You may not notice, but often what you wear reflects
your mood. If you're feeling down, try dressing in the
things you'd usually wear when you're feeling upbeat,
and you may find your mood improves! Look out for what
sorts of colours and prints other people are wearing to
gauge how they are feeling too.

# Chapter 20

*Monday 2.30 a.m.*

I've just got back from Talullah's party. I have overdosed on marshmallows and pizza, but it has been worth it.

I arrived with my make-up bag, hairdryer, straighteners and a selection of some of my fanciest clothes and jewellery.

Mum gave me a hand over the road and a huge unexpected hug on the Banks' doorstep. 'This is very kind of you,' she said. 'Mrs Banks told me it means the world to Talullah.'

I had just gone upstairs, said hello to the girls, eaten my first marshmallow, and got my make-up brushes out, when the doorbell rang.

'Are you expecting anyone else?' I asked them.

They looked at each other and grinned but shook their heads. I heard Mrs Banks opening the door.

A moment later I heard the thunderous pounding of more than one person hurtling up the stairs.

'Where are you, Carrie?' I heard a familiar voice call out.

'Get back, I'm going in first.'

'No, I am!'

Rani, Chloe and Maddy burst into the room all at once.

'Did I hear there was a makeover going on in this house?' Rani cried, holding the others back by stretching out her arms, over one of which hung her huge make-up bag. 'A makeover? Without us?'

'What *were* you thinking?' Chloe shook her head. I could see she was carrying a large bag of accessories and clothes.

'You know you can't possibly have one without me,' Rani scolded. 'You know how it works. *I* do hair and make-up . . .'

'*I* do clothes . . .' Chloe went on.

'And Carrie does general styling and interior design, and I take photos,' Maddy finished. She produced a camera and took a snap. 'And obviously I must also never leave the three of you on your own again because just look what a mess you got yourselves into.'

'I'm *so* glad Gregg came back, Chloe. I'm so sorry . . .' I started.

'Shut up and give me a hug. Give all of us a hug,' said Chloe.

So we all hugged and cried and hugged and cried again.

'Chloe's right,' Rani said. 'Honestly, it wasn't any fun hanging out without you, and when we saw what you were prepared to do to make things right . . .'

'What do you mean?' I asked.

Rani rummaged in her bag and slapped a magazine down. There were several photos of the red carpet at a West End premiere. Brad Pitt was in one, Paige was in another, not looking pleased, and the third one was mainly taken up with a large pair of Union Jack pants and the determined face of the security guard who had me slung over his shoulder.

I knew I shouldn't have worn that mini-skirt.

Chloe produced another magazine with a picture of a startled Gregg having a letter waved in his face. Chloe began to read, '*A crazed Gregg Madison fan broke through the security barriers at the West End premiere of* The Calm. *Determined to deliver her fan letter, it was anything* but *calm as security chased the girl down the red carpet before catching her and carrying her off.'*

'Your mother must be so proud,' Rani said solemnly.

I pulled a face at her and we all burst out laughing.

'How *is* Gregg?' I asked Chloe.

She sat down on the bed, leaned back and sighed. 'Wonderful! But he's mad with Mona for not telling him she saw me.'

She saw me blush and indicated for me to sit down next to her on the bed. 'Don't worry, he's not mad with you. He really understands why you weren't so crazy about us getting together. He appreciated that Tom is very special to you and also that you'd be pretty wary of me going out with someone famous. He did appreciate that in your bonkers way you did it because you cared.'

'And I dooo!' I howled.

'We know.' Rani grinned. 'It took us a few days to get it, plus realising we couldn't survive without you.'

'Nothing was the same.' Chloe squeezed my hand. 'Boyfriends may come and go but girl friends, well, they are forever, aren't they?' Rani said.

'Do you think you'll all be friends when you're little old ladies?' Florence asked.

We looked at each other.

'Yes,' we chorused.

'Well,' said Tallulah, 'are we going to have a makeover party or not? What are you waiting for?'

Mrs Banks' head appeared round the bedroom door.

'Sorry to interrupt, Talullah, but it seems you've got a few more guests . . .'

Emma, Prema, April, Nicki, Jeremy and, lastly, a sheepish-looking Shanaid squeezed into the already-crowded room.

'Hi, Talullah, hi, Florence,' April said. 'I hope it's still OK that we came . . .'

Talullah looked at them all for a moment.

'It's fantastic you came!' she yelled suddenly, jumping up and down. 'Now the party can really begin!'

And it did. And Jeremy didn't object at all to being made up, and I have to say Rani and Chloe did a brilliant job on him. And everyone else.

When I came out on to the landing for a breather I found Talullah, dressed in Chloe's silver mini with sequins, finishing a call on her mobile.

'Who were you calling?' I asked. I am turning into my mother.

'Donna. I asked Shanaid for her number.'

'What did you say?'

'Shanaid said that Donna genuinely felt bad about what happened when she realised how serious it was and that she has a pretty awful life with her sister and mother. Apparently her mum's not very nice . . .'

Having seen Donna's mother and the critical, sneering way she sometimes spoke to Jet I knew that this was true.

'So I asked her if she wanted to come over. She said she didn't think she would feel right coming tonight, but she's going to come round another time, when there are fewer people.'

I stared at her. 'You are a very extraordinary girl, Talullah.'

'I know,' she sighed. I caught her eye and she grinned back and grabbed my arm.

'We'd both better get back to all our many, *many* friends,' she giggled.

I took her arm. 'Yes *we* should.' And led her back into the party.

And now I'm writing this in my own bedroom, with my trusty torch.

And if I shine it around the room I can see the mounds of duvet which cover the sleeping forms of Rani, Maddy and Chloe on the floor.

### 3.00 a.m.

Chloe said, 'I'm glad you woke me up. Being woken up by someone blinding me with a torch is one of my very favourite things. But actually now I'm awake – I forgot to tell you something. Something Gregg said.'

'What?'

'It's a message from Gus to you. He's very keen to get the double-dating started, and how are you fixed for next weekend?'

'Tell him I'm having root canal treatment.'

'I'm free.' Rani's voice came from the duvet in the corner.

'No you're not!' Chloe and I both said at once.

'I'm sure I don't know what you mean . . .' Rani replied coyly.

'We all saw you meeting Tallulah's brother earlier,' Maddy joined in.

'Talk about love at first sight!' I sighed.

'Chemistry or what?' Chloe giggled. 'When are you seeing him?'

'Tomorrow. He's going to help me get my Bunsen burner

going,' Rani said seriously.

The room collapsed into howls of laughter.

'Chloe?' I asked once the room was quiet again.

'What now?'

'How's it going to work . . .you know, with you and Gregg?'

'We-ell, he says Mona is so scared he'll fire her that she says she's going to get me an agent and sort out some modelling work! Both here and in America.'

'That's great,' I said.

'Will you miss us?' Rani's voice was small.

'Nope, I'll be much too busy being rich and famous to bother about you lot any more.'

I heard a pillow being thrown and a muffled cry of protest.

'Come on!' Chloe cried. 'You're my forever friends.'

'I don't know what that means, but pass the sick bag.' Rani likes to pretend that she's not sentimental.

'Yes, you do. We'll meet loads of people in our lives, but we will always be there for each other. Come what may. Including boyfriends.'

And I'm smiling as I write this under my duvet. Because I know she's right.

**EVERYONE'S TIP:** •••••••••••••••••••

Keep mementos, tickets, photos, notes, letters and magazine cuttings from your day to day life and stick them in a keepsake book. Date them and add any funny notes or comments – you can get your friends to put some in too. You'll treasure these memories every time you look back over them.

To find out about the Style Sister series,
style tips and lots more, log on to:

**piccadillypress.co.uk/stylesisters**

# The Style Sisters series

## Friends Forever

Carrie realises that she has neglected her friends in favour of a boy and that it's time to change. It's time to become A Better Person.

Befriending the scary new girl at school, match-making and giving her classmates style tips are all part of the plan. But things don't go quite as she expects . . .

## Paris Princess

Carrie, Rani, Chloe and Maddy feel they are going to learn some real style when French exchange students come to stay. But expensive face cream and designer clothes prove to be of little protection from the insecurities and stresses of teen life, as Marie-Camille – a total fashionista princess – pushes Carrie to breaking point.

## Green Goddesses

A new teacher at Boughton High impresses all the girls with his idealistic views and green principles – not to mention his long dark hair and manly six-foot-two frame. As the boys become more than a little jealous, the Year Nine field trip turns out to have more drama and surprises than anyone could have expected!